"Be My Bride. Live With Me. Let Me...Take Care Of You."

"You just don't want to admit you made a mistake," Cassie said, her voice husky. "You think because you're married, however...accidental that marriage was, you should stay married. Stubborn."

"Consistent," Gideon corrected.

"But you don't want to be married to me."

"Don't I?" When his fingertips made a little circle on her arm, his knuckles grazed the side of her breast.

Oh my. "Gideon? I have to know what you want from this marriage." Sex? she thought wildly. Was sex enough to begin a marriage with? Could she accept it if that was all he wanted from her?

Could she refuse?

Dear Reader,

A sexy fire fighter, a crazy cat and a dynamite heroine—that's what you'll find in *Lucy and the Loner*, Elizabeth Bevarly's wonderful MAN OF THE MONTH. It's the next in her installment of THE FAMILY McCORMICK series, and it's also a MAN OF THE MONTH book you'll never forget—warm, humorous and very sexy!

A story from Lass Small is always a delight, and *Chancy's Cowboy* is Lass at her most marvelous. Don't miss out as Chancy decides to take some lessons in love from a handsome hunk of a cowboy!

Eileen Wilks's latest, *The Wrong Wife*, is chock-full with the sizzling tension and compelling reading that you've come to expect from this rising Desire star. And so many of you know and love Barbara McCauley that she needs no introduction, but this month's *The Nanny and the Reluctant Rancher* is sure to both please her current fans…and win her new readers!

Suzannah Davis is another new author that we're excited about, and *Dr. Holt and the Texan* may just be her best book to date! And the month is completed with a delightful romp from Susan Carroll, *Parker and the Gypsy*.

There's something for everyone. So come and relish the romantic variety you've come to expect from Silhouette Desire!

Lucia Macro

Lucia Macro
And the Editors at Silhouette Desire

Please address questions and book requests to:
Silhouette Reader Service
U.S.: 3010 Walden Ave., P.O. Box 1325, Buffalo, NY 14269
Canadian: P.O. Box 609, Fort Erie, Ont. L2A 5X3

EILEEN WILKS
THE WRONG WIFE

SILHOUETTE *Desire*

Published by Silhouette Books

America's Publisher of Contemporary Romance

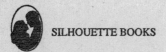 SILHOUETTE BOOKS

ISBN 0-373-76065-5

THE WRONG WIFE

Books by Eileen Wilks

Silhouette Desire

The Loner and the Lady #1008
The Wrong Wife #1065

EILEEN WILKS

is a fifth-generation Texan. Her great-great-grand-mother came to Texas in a covered wagon shortly after the end of the Civil War—excuse us, the War Between the States. But she's not a full-blooded Texan. Right after another war, her Texan father fell for a Yankee woman. This obviously mismatched pair proceeded to travel to nine cities in three countries in the first twenty years of their marriage, raising two kids and innumerable dogs and cats along the way. For the next twenty years they stayed put, back home in Texas again—and still together.

Eileen figures her professional career matches her nomadic upbringing, since she tried everything from drafting to a brief stint as a ranch hand—raising two children and any number of cats and dogs along the way. Not until she started writing did she "stay put," because that's when she knew she'd come home.

This one is for my mother,
wherever she is on her journey

One

There was a head on the pillow next to hers.

Cassandra O'Grady blinked sleepily at the back of a man's head so close to her own. She wasn't alarmed by the sight. Cassie never felt much of anything except reluctance when a new day first forced itself on her. If she'd been capable of thinking yet, though, she might have been amazed at how little she grudged opening her eyes this morning.

She knew that head. But whose leg was cuddled so cozily between hers?

That question had an important ring to it. Cassie's three functioning brain cells—the ones left on, like a night-light, to lead her back to wakefulness—stirred with feeble interest. She blinked and managed to frown.

It was a nice head. Not too round or square or oblong. Just right. The hair covering it in back, her present viewing angle, was nice, too—soft and thick. In the early-morning light, with the rest of the world's colors just starting to wake, that hair held on to the darkness of midnight. Cassie's frown softened into a smile.

Morning, afternoon or night, Gideon's hair was beautiful.

Gideon?

Cassie actually felt her heart start. It made a sudden jump and then began to thump so obviously against the wall of her chest, that she understood that the ignition had just been turned on and the accelerator pressed.

Gideon. Gideon Wilde. That was *Gideon's* head lying on a pillow eight inches from her own.

Oh, yes, she knew the shape of his head, the darkness of his hair and the way his short, no-nonsense haircut left the nape of his neck bare. And those were his wide shoulders flowing into the strong lines of his back, lines she'd sketched only from memory because she couldn't let him know his body fascinated her. That was *Gideon's* back, because Gideon was lying on his stomach beside her in this large, strange bed, stretched out like the big cat she'd often thought he resembled. And though her line of sight didn't go any farther, like beneath the sheet, logic suggested that the leg pressed so intimately between hers belonged to Gideon, too. Gideon's strong, hairy, muscular thigh pressed right up against—

Embarrassment was one type of heat that flooded Cassie as she realized what she wasn't wearing. The same thing he wasn't wearing. Memory rushed in, along with another sort of heat—memories of yesterday…and last night.

She remembered taking Gideon's phone call yesterday at her brother's office. She'd gone with Ryan to meet Gideon at the Blue Parrot Lounge. She remembered the hours at the Blue Parrot and the trip to the airport, followed by the garish lights of the Las Vegas strip…and last night. Oh, yes, she did remember last night.

Beyond the masculine shoulders that partially blocked her view, Cassie could see the pale, gilded colors of the luxury suite, colors that made her think of Cinderella's coach. At the foot of the bed was a Disney version of a pirate's foot locker, painted a soft, dreamy color. Titanium white, she thought, with just enough Hansa yellow to turn milk to cream. Her bouquet rested there. The orchids were a richer cream than the chest they lay upon, and the roses were a paler blush than the color that swept over her as she remembered.

Oh, yes, this was a morning like none before in her life. Cassie smiled, aching with happiness, and started to cuddle closer to the big man in bed with her.

Her movement made him stir. A deep, low, dying sort of groan rumbled up from his chest. He rolled away from her, onto his back, throwing out a heavy arm that glanced off Cassie's chin.

"Ow!"

His eyes jerked open. They immediately squeezed closed again. He made a soft, piteous sound.

She knew Gideon had put away a lot of alcohol yesterday, both before he called her brother and later. She knew Gideon seldom drank more than a single highball and that he probably felt lousy. But he still ought to be more careful what he did with his arms. Cassie frowned, rubbed her chin and scooted back another couple inches.

His eyes opened again. Slowly his head turned on the pillow. From a distance of a foot and a half she looked at Gideon's craggy face, stared right into his unfocused eyes. He looked awful. Well, Gideon never looked really awful, but he did make her think of the Marlboro Man coming off a binge, with his eyes dark as sin and the most beautiful mouth she'd ever seen on a man. Gideon usually managed to present himself to the world as cool, civilized and in charge. The polished veneer helped him deal with the money people who invested in the oil and gas deals he put together.

Not this morning, though. This morning his sophisticated image was ruined by his poor, reddened eyes and the dark stubble of his beard.

She smiled at him tremulously. "Good morning," she whispered.

His eyes widened, then froze in an expression of absolute horror. "Oh, my God."

She almost got away.

Gideon's reactions were slowed by guilt and the worst hangover of his life. Cassie and the sheet made it to the edge of the bed before his sluggish brain caught on to the fact that she was leaving him and taking the covers. And he was naked. Naked and in bed with his best friend's little sister.

He grabbed the end of the sheet and pulled. She fell back onto the bed, her breath whooshing out. The mattress bounced from her weight. He managed not to throw up. He closed his aching eyes, tucked the corner of the sheet around his hips, and lay very still, praying that she'd be still, too.

After a moment the room and his stomach stopped pitching, though the construction crew restructuring his skull from the inside out didn't take a break. He realized Cassie hadn't moved, hadn't said a word since he'd recaptured the sheet she'd been trying to escape with.

The attempted escape had been typical Cassie—all emotion and impulse. This stillness and silence was not. "Cassie," he muttered without opening his eyes. The sound of his voice bounced around painfully inside his head. "I'm sorry." Sorry? At the moment he hated himself more than he'd ever hated anyone in his life. Even his father. "I don't— Whatever happened, I'm sorry."

"Whatever happened?" Her voice was thin, high. "You don't remember?"

The construction crew in his head had his mental landscape all torn up. He tried to sort through the fragments, tried to grasp how he could be here. How could he be in bed with *Cassie?* It was supposed to be Melissa....

But Melissa had dumped him. Four days before the wedding Melissa had called him and rather hysterically backed out.

Gideon had not taken it well. He felt it still, the anger, the bewilderment. Gideon was used to wresting what he wanted from life. He'd wanted to marry Melissa. After getting to know him, she hadn't wanted to marry him. He still didn't know *why.*

"I called Ryan," he said, remembering. He'd been at the

Blue Parrot yesterday, and after a few drinks he'd decided to hold a wake for the dreams Melissa had tossed out the window when she'd rejected him.

The wedding that didn't take place was the first important failure of Gideon's life. He'd planned that wedding for years, since long before he met Melissa, and he was a man who accomplished what he set out to do. Hadn't he reached every other important goal he'd set, from his college degree to his current financial success? But he'd failed at the most important goal, the one that all the others were supposed to lead up to— finding a woman, the right woman, who would marry him and give him what he had no way of getting for himself. A home.

When he'd thought of a wake, naturally he'd called Ryan O'Grady.

But Ryan's little sister had come with him, little Cassie with the short, fiery hair and fey eyes. "He shouldn't have brought you," Gideon said now, harsh with the onslaught of fear because he couldn't *remember*—which meant he'd gotten much more drunk than he'd intended. He'd lost control. And Gideon *never* lost control. "What the hell was Ryan thinking of?"

"Drinking," she said tartly. "That's what you wanted, wasn't it? Someone to get drunk with. So I came along to do the driving and keep the two of you out of trouble."

That's what she always used to say, back when she was a skinny little nuisance trying to tag along with the two college-age boys—that they needed her to keep them out of trouble. Of course, neither of them wanted to avoid trouble at that age. He used to call her… "Mermaid," he said with rough affection. Those memories, at least, were untouched.

"Don't call me that! Not after—not when you don't remember!"

He flinched. Not after last night. Not after he, apparently, got so damned drunk he took his best friend's sister to some damned hotel room and then took her to bed.

There had been a time, shortly after Cassie turned sixteen, when he'd been terrified that something like this would happen—when he'd been unable to keep his body from reacting to the sweet, new curves of a girl much too young for the lechery his mind kept picturing. But Gideon always did what had to be done. He'd learned to control his mind; eventually he'd even subdued the worst of his body's responses, so that he'd been able to be around little Cassie without fearing he'd do something to frighten her or destroy his friendship with her or her brother.

Yet now... "How could Ryan let me do this?" he groaned. "Where the hell was your brother?"

"Don't you remember anything?" Now her voice sounded thick with tears. "It was his idea."

It was *what?* Gideon's eyes popped open as he jerked to a sitting position. The construction crew promptly drove two burning stakes through his eyeballs. He flopped back down and breathed. Slowly. Carefully. And more pieces of the day before fell into place.

Ryan's idea. It had been Ryan's idea to charter the plane when there weren't any commercial flights available. Or had that part been Gideon's contribution? He wasn't sure. He had drunk so damned much he'd lost pieces of his life. Gideon had to wrestle with self-loathing before he could turn his attention to the memories he did have.

Absurdly, the first memory that floated to the surface was of a pirate ship, complete with cannons blazing and men wielding cutlasses. And another ship, a frigate, and a battle between the two that took place...in front of a hotel?

Fireworks, not cannon fire. That's what he'd seen, a carefully staged extravaganza. He remembered going inside the hotel, where the huge lobby gleamed with gold fixtures and a floor shiny enough to see yourself in. And he remembered Cassie's body, slim and warm, tucked up against his as they walked into that hotel lobby. He hadn't wanted to let her go even for a minute, because she might change her mind.

He remembered a taxi ride, and Cassie's face, pale with nerves. The fare had been twelve dollars. He'd given the cabbie a twenty and asked him to wait.

"Vegas," he said quietly. "We're in Las Vegas."

Her silence was confirmation enough. Or almost enough. After a long pause, he made himself move, propping up on one elbow. The jackhammers went crazy inside his head. He ignored them.

He looked down at Cassie's triangular face. Even first thing in the morning her hair was too short and fine to hold a curl or a tangle. It framed her unhappy face in a fringe the color of sunrise. Her chameleon eyes were as gray as rain at the moment, and shiny with tears. Before this morning he would have sworn those eyes were as true and guileless as Cassie herself.

The twist of disillusionment went deep.

His gaze drifted down her slender neck to smooth, white shoulders speckled with a few pale freckles. Impossibly, his body stirred at the sight, which drew his brows together in a tighter scowl. Deliberately he looked from her shoulders to her small breasts, covered by the sheet she clutched tightly in place, and let his eyes linger on the slim gold band on the third finger of her left hand.

Finally he looked back at her face. "Congratulations, Mrs. Wilde," he said bitterly. "A few others have tried to trick their way into sharing the name that goes on my bank statements, but I wasn't expecting it from you. How much will it cost me to buy my way out of this mess?"

She reared up and punched him in the nose.

When Cassie stood under the hot spray of the shower six minutes later she was still shocked at herself. She'd never hit anyone before. Well, not since the fifth grade, anyway, when Sara Sue Leggett had told everyone Cassie got her clothes from the Dumpster behind the Salvation Army.

She ought to feel guilty. She really should. The man obviously had a wretched hangover, and she'd hit him.

Oh, she hoped his nose bled and bled. She just wished she could use up all the hot water so that he'd have to take a cold shower, but that was hard to do in a Las Vegas luxury hotel.

Las Vegas. Cassie bit her lip and poured shampoo into her palm from the little bottle the hotel furnished.

She'd known he might have regrets this morning, but she hadn't known he could look at her the way he had. In the sixteen years since Ryan brought Gideon Wilde home with him from college for the first time, Cassie had seen Gideon's face ice over like that before. He didn't suffer fools gently, and he despised dishonesty. His scorn could be as withering as winter's first frost. But he'd never turned that expression on her before. Not on her. She hadn't expected that.

The shampoo smelled of almonds and lathered beautifully. It was, she noticed, a more expensive brand than she normally bought. Cassie sighed and ran her thumb over the unfamiliar ring on the third finger of her left hand. Gideon thought she'd married him so she could afford a better brand of shampoo.

How could she have been so stupid? How could she have let those two talk her into this?

They'd been at the Blue Parrot, a dinky little bar where Ryan and Gideon used to hang out during their impoverished college days. Maybe the location, with its nostalgic associations, had been partly responsible for the turn the conversation took. Ryan had grown increasingly Irish and sentimental as the afternoon waned into evening, and both men had put away a great deal more liquor than they normally would have.

But Cassie suspected that Ryan had drunk less than Gideon, while encouraging him to drink more. He'd gotten that crafty look in his eyes after the first couple of drinks, the expression that said he thought he was being sly…an expression that usually meant disaster was on its way. Her brother was about as successfully sneaky as a grizzly bear, a big, red-haired grizzly, who created the most havoc when he tried to tiptoe up on a problem instead of charging it with gleeful, bearlike rage. No, subtlety was not a virtue that ran in their family. But Ryan had never seemed to grasp how poor he was at it.

Gideon, unfortunately, had been a bit too intoxicated by then to recognize that gleam in Ryan's eye.

"I have to kill him," Cassie muttered, scrubbing her scalp

vigorously. Her brother loved her. She knew he did. He also drove her crazy. Their father had died when Cassie was little, leaving their mother to raise them as best she could on split shifts and a waitress's income. Ryan, six years older than Cassie, had appointed himself in charge of his sister's life from that day on.

Until yesterday. Yesterday, he'd decided to put someone else in charge of taking care of Cassie—his best friend, Gideon, who needed a woman with more staying power than the blond icicle he'd been engaged to. A loyal woman. A woman, Ryan had emphasized, who could cook.

Cassie had tried hitting him at that point, but even drunk, Ryan's reflexes were better than hers.

At least, she thought as the hot water rinsed the suds from her hair, *my brother stopped short of pointing out just why he thought I'd go along with his stupid idea.* He knew, though. He'd known for years and years.

She considered letting him live.

Of course, Ryan had probably only kept quiet because he knew that her feelings would register on the minus side of Gideon's ledger, not the plus. Gideon did not trust strong feelings. He was emotionally frozen, in fact, which made him exactly the wrong sort of man for Cassie. She needed someone warm and loving, someone who could return all the feelings she longed to pour out. She'd forced herself to face that fact years ago...in her head, at least.

Surely, she thought, scowling at the fogged glass door of the tub enclosure, if she'd had any illusions left, Gideon had shattered them with that sorry excuse for a proposal yesterday. Unlike her brother, Gideon got quiet and serious when he drank. He'd listened gravely to Ryan's heavy-handed suggestions for a substitute bride, then turned to Cassie and announced—not asked, but announced—"We can fly to Vegas tonight. That way I can still get married on my wedding day."

Of course she'd said no. Lord, saying no had been easy. Not painless, but easy. Only somehow she'd wound up here, anyway, naked in Las Vegas with Gideon's ring on her finger.

And, she noticed with a wince as she soaped her body, with an unaccustomed tenderness in a very private place.

She was not going to cry. She'd given up crying for Gideon Wilde eight years ago, when she'd humiliated herself as thoroughly as a woman could. Well, she'd almost given it up. She'd had a minor relapse when she'd heard about the Icicle six months ago, but that didn't really count. She couldn't hold that night against herself.

Oh, but she could hold last night against herself. Last night, when he'd been drunk, hot and hasty…and this morning, when he hated her. She could blame herself for this morning.

No more, she told herself, shutting off the shower that would never run out of hot water no matter how long she stayed in. She'd made a mistake, a huge mistake, letting her brother convince her to listen to the man she'd been in and out of love with since she was twelve.

Not love, she corrected herself. Lust. She could not possibly love a man who didn't remember their wedding night. Her problem, she decided, as she dried off with a towel twice the size any she owned, was that her hormones had gotten themselves fixed on Gideon from an early age, almost as soon as she started having hormones. Somehow, in spite of trying, she'd never gotten them straightened out.

It was time to grow up. Gideon was always so damned cool and rational. He'd selected his fiancée that way, according to Ryan. Logically. Miss Melissa Southwark was everything Gideon wanted. She had the chilly, blond perfection that Cassie knew, with the painful certainty of experience, Gideon preferred in a woman.

Well, Cassie could be logical, too. She'd get her hormones straightened out, along with the rest of her. From this moment on, Cassie would be a different woman. Calm. Rational. In control.

First she had to undo last night's mistake. But to undo a marriage…*divorce* was such an ugly word, and they'd only been married one night. Really, when you thought about it coolly and logically, one night didn't count.

An annulment, she thought, zipping herself back into the jeans she'd been married in, would be best. Although it might not be easy to convince Gideon of that truth. If there was one area where he wasn't always rational, it was what, in another age, would have been called his honor. Gideon didn't lie, and he didn't go back on his word. Ever.

What she had to do, she realized, as she pulled on yesterday's wrinkled silk blouse, was persuade him the contract they'd entered into was not binding. How could she…

When inspiration struck, Cassie smiled, delighted with herself. Unfortunately she wasn't looking in the mirror at that moment. If she had been, she might have recognized the gleam in her eyes, since it strongly resembled her brother's expression when he was at his craftiest. Just before he really messed things up.

"You've got to be kidding," Gideon said. He stood by the closed drapes in their room, wearing a scowl along with yesterday's clothes.

Gideon hated to be rumpled and dirty. He hated the sour taste in his mouth, too, the faint stink of liquor clinging to his shirt and the pounding of his head. Cassie had hidden in the shower a long time, yet room service still hadn't managed to appear with the coffee, aspirin, breakfast and clean clothes Gideon craved. And he hadn't managed to come up with more than fragments of the night before. One of those fragments included a bed, darkness, Cassie…and a vivid, tactile memory of overwhelming lust. That fragment stood alone, banked on either side by foggy nothing. He couldn't remember.

His memory, or lack of it, didn't excuse him. But as far as he could see, his new bride lacked even the feeble excuse of drunkenness for what she had done to him. Cassie had known he was drunk. She'd known what kind of woman he needed— hadn't he told her and Ryan both, while drinking toasts to the wedding that didn't happen? Yet she'd married him anyway.

He scowled at her.

Cassie marched to the window where he stood and seized

the drapery pull. "I hope breakfast gets here soon, Gideon. Your blood sugar must be low. It's interfering with your reason. Of course we'll get the marriage annulled." She yanked on the cord, flooding the room with hideously bright light that the white sheers did nothing to tame. "There, that's better. Mornings in the desert are beautiful, aren't they?"

Gideon winced at the assault on his abused eyeballs. The sunshine lit a fire in Cassie's hair, a fire that should have clashed with the tomato-red silk of the blouse she wore tucked into her jeans but didn't. Vivid colors suited Cassie as pastels never would.

Melissa, Gideon thought, his scowl deepening, would never wear a shirt that bright. Melissa preferred soft blues and peaches that didn't overwhelm her delicate blond coloring. She wouldn't have opened those drapes without asking, either. He was sure of it. "There's nothing wrong with my reason. Yours, however—" Patience, he reminded himself, was necessary to maintaining control. "Cassie, you must know an annulment isn't possible after the marriage has been consummated."

"So?" She propped her hands on her hips in a familiar, challenging pose.

"Obviously, after last night—"

"I thought you didn't remember last night."

The shock of fear over his loss—of memory, of control— was less than it had been. Less, but still powerful. "I don't," he said, his voice flat with the effort of detachment. "But when I wake up naked, in bed with a woman who is also naked, I don't need an instant replay to tell me what happened the night before."

"Well," she said, "I hate to tell you this, but you had an awful lot to drink yesterday, Gideon. You're not used to that. You mustn't be upset that your, ah, manly functions were impaired."

"My *what?*"

"You know what I mean."

"Are you saying that I didn't—that I passed out?"

"Not exactly. You tried. It isn't as if you didn't try. You

just *couldn't.*" She stepped closer and patted his arm. The gold band on her finger winked at him mockingly in the sunshine. "It's okay, though. Really."

He stepped back and glared.

She smiled sweetly at him. "Don't worry. I'm sure there's no permanent problem. And an annulment is much tidier than a divorce, don't you think?"

The knock at the door pleased Gideon. Thinking of coffee and a clean shirt, tabling consideration of Cassie's bombshell, he strode to the door and opened it without hesitating.

The man on the other side of the door was very like Gideon, and very different. The expressions the two men faced each other with were identically grim, but the newcomer's scowling mouth was framed by a thick mustache. He was every bit as tall as Gideon, and even heavier through the chest and shoulders. Where Gideon's hair was the limitless black of midnight, this man's hair flamed with sunrise.

Just like Cassie's.

"I want to talk to my sister," the other man growled. "Now."

Gideon sighed. Of course Ryan showed up before Gideon's coffee and clean shirt did, and of course he was breathing fire. On a morning like this, what else could he expect? Gideon stepped back, silently holding the door open for the one man he considered a friend—or had. Until this morning.

Ryan charged into the room. "Cassie," he said as he reached for her. "Cassie—"

She held an arm out stiffly, as if that slender limb could really hold off her oversize brother, and announced, "I am going to kill you this time."

Ignoring her arm and her statement equally, he grabbed her shoulders, peering into her face. "Are you all right?"

She rolled her eyes. "No, I've been ravished too many times to count. Quit playing—"

The growl rumbling up from Ryan's chest didn't sound playful. Gideon went from standby to full alert.

Cassie grabbed her brother's arm and hung on as he turned

to face Gideon. "I am not going to have this, do you hear me? You are not going to pound on Gideon. Yesterday you did everything but offer him some cows and ponies if he'd take me off your hands, and now you come barging in here as if he'd abducted me! What in the world is wrong with you—other than the usual, I mean?"

Ryan didn't bother to look sheepish. "Yesterday I'd had too much to drink. That doesn't—"

"Doesn't excuse you in any way, form or fashion! What I want to know is—" Cassie broke off to stare at Gideon. "Would you mind?" she asked irritably. "I'd like to talk to Ryan privately for a minute."

He could, he thought, take offense at having his bride of nine hours ask him to go away and let her talk with her brother privately. He could have been amused. He'd often been amused in the past by the way the pair of O'Gradys interacted with each other—alternately quarrelsome and affectionate, full of dire threats and a fierce, unshakable loyalty.

Today he simply felt the chill and the distance. He'd never known how to belong like that. "You know," he said, surprising himself, "I think I do mind."

The knock that landed on the still-open door was a welcome interruption. Room service had arrived at last.

Two

Brother and sister argued in vehement whispers while the waiter set out a variety of breakfast dishes. Gideon didn't go to the bathroom for the shower and clean clothes he badly needed. For some reason he simply did not want to leave the room.

He watched as Ryan helped himself to a cup of coffee and Cassie picked up one of the croissants and tore the end off, neither of them bothering to sit down. He could hear snippets of their argument as he signed the tab and tipped the waiter, enough to know that, as angry as Cassie was with him, she was still trying to persuade Ryan he shouldn't blame Gideon for yesterday's events.

Gideon couldn't remember anyone ever defending him. His response was swift and physical. The sting of desire was sharp enough to burn, strong enough to disorient him.

He wanted Cassie. Badly. He was still angry over all he'd lost by marrying the wrong woman, angry with her as well as himself. He still felt betrayed in a private corner of his soul no one had ever managed to disturb before. But he wanted her with bewildering intensity.

He watched her argue with her brother. Cassie put her whole body behind everything she said, everything she did. Like a candle flame, he thought—always in motion. She wasn't beautiful the way Melissa was. She was short and slight and…fascinating. The sleeves of her silk blouse were rolled up, and the pale flesh of her arms gesturing fluidly enticed him as if she'd bared her breasts. He felt ridiculous. And aroused.

Maybe he didn't consciously remember what had happened between them last night, but his body remembered. If, as she'd said, he hadn't been able to finish what he started, then he might want her all the more today because of what he hadn't done last night.

If he could have her even once, he thought, the hunger wouldn't be so keen, so consuming. He could regain control.

He watched as Cassie grabbed the butter knife. She paused in her vehement discussion long enough to spread a precise amount of pale, creamy butter on the end of the croissant. She was such an odd little creature. In some ways she subsisted on impulse and emotion as purely as fire lives off the oxygen it burns, yet in others she was as neat and orderly as the facets of a crystal—a small, tidy agent of chaos.

He had never pretended to understand her. He watched her now, but he was remembering a skinny girl with messy braids and eldritch eyes.

Gideon had gone home with his new roommate for a rare weekend off. Not that he'd planned to. At eighteen, Gideon hadn't thought he had time for friendships, not with his heavy course load and the part-time job his aunt considered an essential part of his college experience. Being the sort of woman she was, Aunt Eleanor had made the job necessary in fact as well as theory. She'd paid for his tuition and books. Everything else was up to him. If Gideon didn't work, he didn't eat.

But Ryan O'Grady, for all that he seemed like a cheerful Irish grizzly, was almost as ambitious, every bit as stubborn, and twice as poor as Gideon was. Eventually Gideon had given in and accepted Ryan's invitation home. By the time the two of them had walked up the short path to the run-down mobile home in a south Dallas trailer park, though, Gideon was regretting having agreed to the weekend.

Not that the poverty bothered him. He'd lived in places a good deal worse before his aunt took him in, places where no one bothered to trim the grass or set out pots of grocery store mums to brighten a tiny front porch like someone had done here. No, he hadn't wanted to be there because he didn't know how to act around a regular family.

"Ryan!" a lilting voice had called out from somewhere above their heads. "I'm so glad you're here! I have to warn you, though." The voice had dropped confidentially. "Mom has been cooking all morning."

Gideon had looked up, right into a mermaid's eyes. A very dirty, landlocked little mermaid, with an elf's pointed face, skinned knees, and braids half undone, sat on the roof of that rundown mobile home, her bare feet dangling, and watched them solemnly.

"Is that bad?" he'd been startled into asking.

She'd nodded. "You have to eat it, you see." She looked him up and down, and her eyes brightened. "You look like you could eat a lot."

"He does," Ryan had said, laughing and lifting his arms. "Eats like a horse. Mom will love him. Come down from there, brat, you're confusing our guest."

Quick as that, she'd drawn her legs up, held her own skinny arms out, and leaned out into thin air, falling right into her brother's arms. Gideon had never forgotten the look on her face as she fell. Trust. Utter, joyous trust.

No, Gideon didn't understand Cassie. Not the little girl he remembered, or the young woman who stood across the room from him now in a gold and white Las Vegas suite, scattering crumbs on the thick carpet while she argued with her brother. But he did understand responsibility.

"Ryan," he said, deciding it was time they settled things. "You didn't come to my room to argue with Cassie."

The other man looked over at him. "No," he agreed slowly. "I came here to see if you needed your bones broken."

Cassie made an impatient noise that the two men ignored. "You thought I would hurt her?" Gideon asked.

"You were drunk," Ryan said bluntly. "So was I, or I wouldn't have let her go with you when you were in that shape."

Gideon nodded, accepting that. "Well?"

Ryan faced him. "She says you didn't hurt her. So the next question is, what do you plan on doing now?"

Gideon was silent. What was he going to do? Until Cassie had come out of the shower and announced her desire for an annulment, his course had seemed clear. He'd made promises. Never mind that he'd been drunk at the time. If anything, that made it even more important that he take responsibility for his actions—financial responsibility, at least. Money was the basis for this marriage, after all, however Cassie might try to deny it now.

Then Cassie had said she wanted an annulment. He couldn't let that happen. Gideon didn't know why it was so important, but he simply could not let her erase their marriage as if it had never happened.

After all, dammit, he *wanted* her. He ached, and the intensity of that ache unsettled him. He realized that one time with her would be not be enough. And didn't Cassie owe him something, too? "I promised her my support," he said slowly, forcing himself to think beyond the throbbing in his loins and the confusion in his mind. A piece of yesterday's jigsaw puzzle floated to the surface. "That was our deal, that I'd support her if she would marry me," he said, remembering. "She wants to paint."

"She *needs* to paint," Ryan corrected. "Not just because of the gallery owner who's interested in the direction she's taken with her work lately. That's important to her career, sure, but painting means more to Cassie than a career."

Cassie frowned and muttered something to her brother. Gideon didn't listen.

He understood what Ryan meant when he said Cassie needed to paint. Painting meant more to her than anything, including the husband she'd acquired in order to pursue her painting. He just hadn't thought Cassie could use people that way. He hadn't thought she could use *him* that way.

Yes, he decided, she did owe him. Chances were, though, her brother wouldn't care for the type of repayment Gideon had in mind. Gideon didn't want to lose Ryan's friendship. He had to set this up carefully. "What I decide has to be up to Cassie to some extent. I'm willing to settle funds on her."

"Marriage involves a hell of a lot more than a checkbook. If you're not—"

"He said it was up to me," Cassie interrupted.

She might as well have not spoken. "What I want to know," Ryan said to Gideon, "is whether you intend to dump my little sister or not. I had my reasons for encouraging this marriage—"

Cassie squawked and grabbed her brother's arm.

"—but that's because I trusted you to take care of her. I'm not talking about money here, Gideon."

Ryan knew better, Gideon thought with a hot flick of resentment. At least Ryan *ought* to know how little Gideon had to offer a woman, other than money. The man had no business insisting on that damned ambiguous "more." But he *was* insisting. And he was Gideon's best friend, maybe his only real friend. Gideon made up his mind suddenly.

Ryan wouldn't like it at all if he knew just what Gideon intended to give Cassie, other than financial support. Gideon didn't plan on enlightening him. "You're right. We should give this marriage a try, at least for a time."

"For a time?" Ryan's eyes narrowed. "Just what does that mean?"

"Yeah," Cassie said, an identical expression on her narrower, more feminine face. "What does that mean?"

"Six months."

Cassie threw up her hands. "You're crazy."

"A year," Ryan said. "Anything less than a year would strike me as insincere."

"All right." Gideon nodded. They wouldn't have to live together the entire time, after all. "At the end of the year, if we're not both convinced the marriage is working out, I can still settle some funds on her."

"Have either of you noticed that I'm right here in the room with you?" Cassie demanded. "Do you two really think I'm going to let you settle my future as if I were a property Gideon didn't want to buy, but is considering leasing? Come on, Ryan, you're supposed to be so hot at real estate. Can't you bargain Gideon up to a two-year lease? And shouldn't we talk about who's responsible for necessary maintenance and repairs? Like dental work. And health insurance. Usually the owner carries structural insurance—I guess that would translate as major medical—while the leaser is responsible for—"

"Come here," Ryan said, and grabbed Cassie's arm. He pulled her, protesting, over by the window, where the two of them carried on another discussion, this time mostly in whispers. But Gideon had excellent hearing. He caught a few stray words, enough to realize that Ryan knew something about Cassie that she wanted kept secret.

Gideon's disillusionment deepened. What could that mean, except that Cassie did, indeed, want his money, and didn't want him to know? Gideon didn't blame Ryan. He'd known, even yesterday when he was drunk, that Ryan was doing his damnedest to manipulate the two of them into this marriage. But Ryan only wanted what was best for his sister. That was how it should be. Brothers, especially older brothers, should look out for their younger sisters...or brothers.

Gideon felt an old, old ache.

Cassie kept darting wary glances at Gideon. Finally she nodded.

"Good," Ryan said, looking relieved. "It's settled, then." He glanced around, noticed the table full of breakfast dishes, and his face lit up. "I haven't eaten yet." He reached for one of the chairs next to the table.

Cassie pushed his hand off the chair. "Nothing is settled, and you're not staying."

"There's plenty of food," Ryan pointed out.

"I'll take it from here. Goodbye, brother." She pushed on his chest. He laughed.

Their tussle was brief. Cassie won it handily in spite of her size, but that had more to do with whatever she hissed in his ear than with brute strength. Ryan sent a last, longing glance at the table of food before he gave up and went to the door, saying he'd see them both back in Dallas. "I'll even call Mom for you," he told Cassie with a grin. "Let her know what you've been up to."

As soon as the door closed behind Ryan, Gideon expected Cassie to launch into whatever harangue she'd been saving up for him. Instead, she stood there next to the door, looking uncertain—an experience that must have been as disconcerting for her as it was for him. Cassie had never been awkward around him before.

It was her own fault if she felt awkward now, he told himself. "Come on," he said. "Let's eat before we try to settle anything else."

They sat opposite each other at the white-draped table. Silence stretched out between them for another minute while Gideon pretended to want the eggs he methodically ate. Cassie spent the whole minute buttering a croissant and not looking at him. Sunshine gleamed off the ornate handle of the butter knife, and off the smooth simplicity of her bright hair. "Gideon," she said at last, setting down the mangled croissant and meeting his eyes. "Gideon, listen to me. I did not marry you because I want, or need, your money."

"Don't." Anger roiled in his stomach, and he set down his fork. "Dammit, Cassie, I know how you grew up, how little money there was and how hard your mother worked to keep a roof over your heads. I can understand you wanting more. God knows I understand that. And you've always been impulsive, so maybe the big surprise is that you've never run off to Vegas before now. Just don't pretend. Dammit, don't pretend!''

Her mouth turned down. "Oh, Gideon. Do you really think so little of women, or yourself? Do you think the only reason a woman would marry you is for your money?''

Her misunderstanding bothered him. He stood. "I'm not down on women, Cassie. The way I see it, men and women are both programmed by our biologies, but the operating systems aren't the same. For a woman, a successful mating is one that provides her and her children with a strong provider. In today's world that translates into money. That isn't wrong, it's just nature at work.''

"A 'successful mating,''' she repeated slowly, taking the napkin from her lap and laying it on the table. "And just what constitutes a 'successful mating' in terms of a man's biology?''

He frowned. He didn't seem to be getting his point across. Her expression made him think of a pot about to boil. "Evolution has geared men toward multiple sexual partners, since that spreads a man's seed—''

She shoved back from the table so hard it wobbled, spilling coffee from Gideon's cup onto the white cloth. "I guess that means last night was thoroughly unsuccessful for both our biologies, then, wasn't it? That,'' she flung at him as she started to pace, "is the most disgusting theory I've ever heard. Of all the self-serving justifications for infidelity, that just about tops the list.''

His eyes followed her as she paced. He'd always thought leprechauns would move the way Cassie did—quick, supple, efficient. "Calm down. I'm not promoting infidelity. Animals are victims of their biology. People aren't. A man who lacks the willpower to keep his word isn't much of a man. After all, men require fidelity from their wives so we'll know whose children we're raising. We have to be prepared to reciprocate.''

She paused in front of the window. The hard, white light

admitted by the gauzy sheers surrounded her like an edgy aura.
"Oh, you do, huh?"

He nodded. "It's only fair. A woman wants to know her
man comes only to her for sex, because sex is a powerful tool
for keeping a male contented. A contented male is more likely
to provide well for his family. Women—"

She screeched in rage.

"—are notoriously emotional about this sort of thing," he
finished, eyeing her cautiously. "But it is really quite logical."

"I am not emotional." She glared at him, her hands fisted
at her sides. "I am reasonable. Calm. Logical. And I'm going
to very reasonably explain to you why all your stupid logic is
a pile of horse manure."

The smile that broke over his face surprised them both. "I
won't be bored," he murmured, mostly to himself. "Whatever
else can be said about this marriage we've gotten ourselves
into for the next year, it won't be boring."

She folded her arms across her chest. "We are not staying
married."

Oh, she was an O'Grady, all right. Stubborn to the core.
But he knew her weakness. "Not indefinitely," he agreed.
"But I've no intention of destroying my friendship with Ryan
by kicking his little sister out the day after the wedding. Even
if that is what you want."

"Ryan wouldn't..." She drifted off uncertainly.

"You know him better than that. Ryan's as good a friend
as a man can have, but his first loyalty is to his family, not to
me. How do you think he'll react if he thinks I've treated you
badly?" He started toward her. "It's not as if I'd blame him,
either. I do remember parts of yesterday afternoon and evening, Cassie. I know what you expect from our bargain.
You've had to spend too much of your time in dead-end jobs
instead of painting." He stopped in front of her. "I told you
I'd give you everything you wanted if you would marry me.
I'm not a man to go back on my word."

Gideon studied the stubborn set of her jaw and decided he
didn't mind her obstinacy. He'd never objected to a challenge.

"I've no intention of letting you go back on your word, either." He moved closer.

She didn't back away, but she wanted to. He could tell by the nervous way her tongue flicked over her lips. "Stop smiling like that," she ordered.

"Like what?"

"Like a cat waiting outside a mouse hole."

His smile broadened. "As I recall, you always liked cats."

"What does that have to do with—" Her breath caught audibly when he moved even closer.

Too close. Gideon stopped with a bare inch between their bodies. If he'd thought to dominate her, to intimidate her with the sheer force of his size, into his way of thinking, that thought fled at the feeling he saw flash across her face.

Desire. Innocent, but not simple, tangled up as it was in the shifting colors of those changeable eyes as she looked up at him, defiant, wary—and obviously unaware of what she'd just given away. And if Cassie's breath had caught with sudden, unwelcome arousal at his nearness, Gideon lost his breath altogether.

She wants me. Cassie wants me.

His world shifted with that realization. Desire turned to need, to an aching imperative. He understood for the first time how a woman could drive a man to his knees…because Cassie, fey little Cassie with the fiery hair, *was* a woman. Not a girl. She was twenty-eight, not sixteen as she had been the first time he'd felt this way, not off limits, not forever inaccessible…oh, no, not inaccessible at all, judging by the look in her eyes.

The predator in Gideon roared to the surface of his brain while heat exploded in his body from the groin outward. *Mine,* he thought, already hard, impossibly ready. He reached out.

Reason didn't rise and reassert itself. The flicker of uncertainty in her eyes didn't keep him from grabbing roughly at what he wanted. Fear did.

His, not hers.

The fear didn't even have to wholly surface to send shock

waves through him. Like a leviathan at the bottom of a lake it stirred, and Gideon's hand faltered just as he touched the place where the silk of her sleeve ended and the silky flesh of her arm began. *I almost lost control,* he thought. With the conscious thought came a dim amazement as the fear settled back into the murk.

Arousal still pulsed through him, making the tips of his fingers extraordinarily sensitive. That must have been why her skin felt so good to him, why he couldn't resist stroking it lightly. He watched her eyes darken in response, and felt a flare of triumph.

She wanted him. He wanted her, too—but he could control his desires. He had to. "Give our agreement a chance, Cassie." He slid his fingers down to her wrist and toyed with the delicate skin over her pulse point. "Be my bride. Live with me. Let me…take care of you."

Cassie's pulse was pounding. She knew Gideon could feel it. She *wanted* him to feel it, wanted, with a power that held her immobile, for him to go on touching her. Easily, naturally, she gave herself up to the feeling. "You just don't want to admit you made a mistake," she said, her voice husky. Cassie saw no contradiction between arguing with him and being aroused by him. "You're not very flexible, Gideon. You think that because you're married, however—" Her breath hitched as his fingers slid back up her arm, dragging tingles behind them like the frothy wake of a boat. "However accidental that marriage was, you think you should stay married. Stubborn."

"Consistent," he corrected. His fingertips slid up under the sleeve of her shirt. The small invasion felt unbearably intimate, as if he'd found some secret place on her body. "I'm a very consistent man."

"It's not logical," she insisted as his fingers trailed around to the inside of her arm…lightly. Ever so lightly. Her skin broke out in goose bumps. "You don't want to be married to me."

His mouth, that beautiful, sensual mouth, tilted up at one

corner. "Don't I?" When his fingertips made a little circle on her arm, his knuckles grazed the side of her breast.

Oh, my. She swallowed so she wouldn't gasp. Or moan. "You were going to marry the Icicle. I mean Melissa. You got drunk because you couldn't marry her."

His fingers stopped moving. His eyes went still with the dark, chill quiet of a frozen pond at night. Deliberately, his eyes fixed on hers, he repeated the motion of a moment before, circling the skin on her arm with his fingertips…circling the side of her breast with his knuckles. "You're not sure if you can trust me, are you, Cassie?"

"It's not very… consistent…of you," she managed to say, "marrying me when you wanted her."

He abandoned the pretense of rubbing her arm. His knuckles skimmed up the side of her breast. "I don't want her now." Slowly his hand went down again. Up.

Helplessly her eyes closed as the undertow caught her, dragging her along like a shellfish tumbled by the tide across a gravelly ocean bed—a rough place in spite of the lightness of his caress, a place of confusion and sharp, conflicting currents.

Those hard, seemingly casual knuckles traced the curve of her breast, dipping under it, coming close to the nipple on the way up. Half of her breast seemed to catch the heat from his hand and reflect it back at him. The other half was cold, aching, bereft. His touch skimmed under her breast, around, closer to the tip, nearly touching it…nearly…circling…

"Gideon——?"

Her own longing forced her eyes open. He wasn't looking at her face anymore. He stared openly at her breasts, at the bumps her nipples made beneath the silk—the nipples he'd made harden, but refused to touch.

She grabbed his wrist. Her breath came hard, as if she'd been running. She didn't know if she was going to shove his arm away or move his hand where she needed it. "What do you want?" she demanded hoarsely. "I have to know what you want from this marriage." *Sex?* she thought wildly. He'd never wanted her before. Maybe his body remembered last night, though, even if his mind didn't, because he wanted her now. Was sex enough to begin a marriage with? Could she accept it, if that was all he wanted from her?

Could she refuse?

Slowly his gaze left her breasts, sliding up again to her face. But she couldn't read anything in his eyes, nothing but the settled darkness that spoke of both passion and control, a mixture Cassie couldn't understand. "One year," he said. "Give me one year to keep my word to you. Then we'll end it."

The pain was sharp enough to send her shooting to the surface. She sucked in air as if she'd actually been underwater, and stepped back. "An annulment would—"

He was shaking his head before she finished getting the word out of her mouth. "No. Not now. Not ever."

Why? Why would he prefer divorce to—unless, she thought with an awakening flick of temper, he wanted to have her in his bed for that year.

That was it, she realized. The man had decided he wanted her, therefore he would have her. *For a year.*

She tried to step back. His hands slid to her waist and stopped her.

His eyes were unfathomable as they met hers. His harsh face gave nothing away, but his hands spread out, claiming more of her. His thumb almost brushed the underside of her breast. Heat arrowed through her, reminding her of passion...and frustration. "I'm not going to agree to an annulment," he said. "Nor to a divorce. Not yet. Will you fight to be free of me, Mermaid?"

His eyes are so dark, she thought. So dark and filled with answers and questions she couldn't guess, reasons and motives he didn't want her to see. But for a moment as his fingers stirred her subtly, powerfully, she thought she saw past the control to the man beneath. A man who wanted her. A man who could be hurt.

"I guess," she said, her voice damnably unsteady, "I'll give it a try."

She saw triumph, quickly masked, flare in Gideon's eyes,

and looked away. She wished she knew just how much of a
fool she was being. How much had he manipulated her? With
his touch, yes—he'd used his skill and her own hunger against
her. She acknowledged that. But the other? Had she seen past
the surface into the vulnerable man beneath—or had he let her
have that glimpse, because on some level he knew that it was
the one sure way to get what he wanted from her?

Three

When the door to Cassie's apartment closed behind her at twelve-thirty that afternoon, she was alone.

Thank God.

She leaned her back against the door and looked at her haven, badly in need of this chance to catch her breath. She'd driven here from the airport, where her car had been parked. Gideon—her *husband*—had taken a limo to his apartment. A place she'd never seen. The place she was supposed to move into this afternoon. A moving company would be here soon to pack up her things, most of which would go into storage. Gideon had insisted on arranging it.

Exhaling with a *whoosh,* she sank to the floor, then just sat there, dazed, looking around the room that had been home for the past five years.

Cassie's one-room apartment took up half of the converted third floor of a narrow old house in a part of Dallas the yuppies and preservationists hadn't gotten around to saving yet. She'd collected its furnishings from flea markets and the occasional going-out-of-business sale. Because she loved textures, she had both wicker and wooden furniture. Because she loved color, both wicker and wood were painted in stained-glass colors, and the braided rug on the oak floor could have competed with Joseph's coat of many colors. A huge, handwoven wall hanging on the north wall mixed feathers, yarn, rope, string and shells in shades of cream, turquoise and rusty red. Floor-to-ceiling shelves held books and other important objects. In one corner her banana-colored sheets and turquoise spread dipped to the floor from the sides of her unmade bed.

She looked at that bed. Only yesterday morning she'd been running late and decided not to make it up before leaving for work. Yesterday morning, when she was still single.

Cassie's room was otherwise clean and tidy. She might thrive on chaos, but order, she firmly believed, had its place, and clean dishes were almost as important as clean paint brushes. Both the tidiness and the mismatched furniture suited her, as did the whole room full of comfortably worn objects—objects that were *hers*. And movers would come today, pack up everything but her clothes and toiletries, and put it all in storage.

She considered blaming her brother for her predicament. He'd pulled her aside in that hotel room and said that it was time to either fish or cut bait. If she wanted Gideon, she had him—for a year. If she didn't want him badly enough to risk trying to keep him, she'd better get serious about getting over him.

Cassie looked at the one unabashedly messy area of the room. Between two windows sat her easel with the newly prepared canvas she'd planned to start on this weekend. Finished paintings leaned against the wall and the legs of the big, ugly table that held her painting supplies. Beneath easel and table stretched a paint-spattered drop cloth.

She thought wistfully that it would be lovely not to have to work. To paint all day. If this were a real marriage... But as things were, there was no way she could just live off Gideon. Maybe she could find something part-time...

Feet thudded on the outside stairs that led up to her apartment. Cassie winced. Her moment of privacy was over. The noisy feet paused at the second floor landing, where Cassie's friend Moses lived. Cassie heard the knock that landed on Mo's door and the husky female voice that called out, "Come on, Mo! Cassie's back. Her car is out front."

With a sigh Cassie pushed to her feet and stepped back from the door. There was no point in protesting the invasion that was about to occur. And they were, after all, her best friends.

The owner of that distinctive female voice hollered, "Come on!" at Mo. In a rushed clatter of feet she arrived at Cassie's door and threw it open without knocking.

"Cassie!" Jaya Duncan stopped just inside the open door, hands on her skinny hips, her full skirts swishing around her ankles from the force of her arrival. "What the hell did you think you were doing, leaving that 'won't be home tonight' message on my machine last night?"

"Keeping you from worrying?" Cassie offered. Knowing Jaya would be singing at the club at that hour, she'd taken thirty seconds to call from the airport. If her message had been rather sparse on details, well, she'd been in a hurry.

"Hah!" Jaya said. "You robbed me of hours of sleep, wondering what you were up to."

Since Jaya was, as usual, vibrating with enough energy for two people, Cassie grinned unrepentantly. "You never bother to tell me when you're going to stay out all night with your passion-of-the-month."

"That's different." Jaya flicked one elegant hand dismissively. "I do that sort of thing. You don't. Besides, you aren't even seeing anyone. So where were you?"

Cassie was granted a brief reprieve when another figure, tall and slim and male, appeared behind Jaya. "Cassie," Mo said, smiling that slow smile of his. "I'm glad to see you got back in one piece, in spite of Jaya's proclamations of disaster."

Cassie smiled back. Her two friends couldn't have made a greater contrast. Mo was quiet and steady, with gentle eyes, a big nose, and a fair complexion that suited his curly blond hair. Jaya's exotic looks came from combining a Hindu mother with a Scots-Irish-Mexican father. Her skin was dusky, her dark hair as thick and glossy as a wig, and she was bossy as all get-out. She and Cassie had been friends since the second grade.

In addition, Jaya was thoroughly, enthusiastically heterosexual. Mo wasn't.

"So where were you?" Mo asked, moving Jaya aside so he could come in.

Cassie sighed. "I was in Vegas, actually," she said. "I got married."

"M-m-married?" Jaya looked from Cassie to Mo and back. "Cassie?"

Cassie nodded and held up her left hand, fingers spread to show her ring.

"Oh, my God."

"Those were Gideon's words," Cassie muttered.

"Gideon," Jaya repeated. "Gideon Wilde. You married him? You actually married Gideon Wilde? Oh, my God."

"Isn't he the man you told me about?" Mo asked. Mo's lover had left him six months ago, about the time Cassie heard about Gideon's engagement. They'd sat up with a couple of bottles of wine and talked their way into morning. "The one who was engaged to someone else?"

She grimaced. "He isn't engaged now. She broke off with him a few days ago."

"Talk about rebound," Jaya said. "I can't believe it. I just can't believe it. You actually married him. How? Where? And you didn't tell me! You didn't even invite me!"

"You were singing at the club by then," Cassie said. "And everything happened so fast—"

"Did you drug him? How did you get him to agree?"

"He asked me," Cassie said, injured. "And I'll have you know I didn't say yes right away, either." It had taken Gideon and Ryan working together almost a whole hour to get her to agree.

It hadn't taken Gideon on his own that long to get her to

set aside her idea of an annulment. Of course, he hadn't exactly played fair about how he persuaded her.

She really ought to be upset about that.

"So what," Mo asked gently, "are you doing here, if you're married?"

"Packing." Cassie bit her lip. Had she really agreed to leave everything she knew for a man who wanted her in his bed for a year? One year...and her brother had had to talk him up from six months.

She moaned and sank down onto the faded candy stripes of her sofa. "And before you ask—no, I don't know what I'm doing. I'm crazy. I've got to be crazy. How did I get myself into this?"

Jaya moved a newspaper folded to the Help Wanted section off the couch, and sat beside her. Mo sat on the other side. "Like usual, I imagine," Jaya said, putting an arm around Cassie's shoulders and squeezing. "You jumped in with both feet, damn the torpedoes and all that stuff. Just like you always do. Now, you tell me all about it. Who were you rescuing this time?"

"No one." Cassie frowned. "Really, Jaya, I'm perfectly capable of minding my own business. I like to help people out sometimes, that's all."

"Whatever you say. Just tell me how you wound up marrying the man you've carried a torch for all these years. And why you're so unhappy about it."

"Not all these years," Cassie protested. "Not continuously, anyway. I got tired of unrequited love when I turned twenty. Remember Randall?"

"Ha!" Jaya waved away the young man responsible for the loss of Cassie's virginity with one scarlet-tipped hand. "That chipmunk doesn't rate as even a minor distraction."

"Randall was cute and sensitive."

"Randall was a nerd."

"Even if you don't count Randall, I haven't exactly been pining away. What about Max?" she demanded, referring to her only other serious involvement, with a baseball player she'd dated two years ago.

"Max is an idiot. A gorgeous idiot, sure, and even a pretty nice guy, which just made it harder for you to admit how much he bored you. He doesn't count."

"Then there's Sam, or J.T., or any number of other guys I've dated—"

"Cassie," Mo interrupted, "Jaya knows, and I know, that you date so many men because you think there's safety in numbers. You like to fix the men you go out with—fix them up with a friend of yours or with a new job or just with a listening ear and good advice. You don't go to bed with them, and you certainly don't run off to Vegas with them. This Wilde is different."

"That's right," Jaya agreed. "The fact is, you've never seriously tried to get Gideon Wilde out of your system. You've just played around at it. Now quit changing the subject, and tell us how you wound up married to him."

So Cassie told them, leaving out a few of the really personal details, like her wedding night and what she'd told Gideon had happened. Or hadn't happened. She wound up talking mostly about the ceremony itself—conducted in the Weddings-To-Go Chapel of Love.

"The three of us were on our way back from the license place," she told them. "It's open until midnight during the week and around the clock on weekends. Anyway, our cab passed this RV with a neon bride on the side, and Gideon flagged it down."

Jaya laughed, and Cassie told her about the minister's rhinestone-studded tuxedo, which had far outshone Cassie's jeans and silk blouse. Mo, she noticed, didn't say much. Finally, with a sigh, Cassie stood. "I've really got to get some things in a suitcase before the movers get here."

"What do you mean 'before the movers get here'?" Jaya went over to the tiny breakfast bar and lifted the lid of the pig-shaped cookie jar by one ear. The jar emitted a loud *oink* as she took out a couple of sandwich cookies.

"She said she was here to pack, Jaya." Mo's frown announced his opinion of her plans.

"But I thought—surely you're not going to *stay* married, are you?" Jaya looked astounded. "I mean, running off to Vegas is a great adventure, but you have to draw the line somewhere. Moving in with the man—" Jaya stopped suddenly and pointed a cookie at Cassie. "Gideon does know you're moving in, doesn't he? You're not planning to just surprise him?"

Mo laughed.

"Good grief! You do think I'm an idiot, don't you? He knows. He gave me his key." She ducked into her walk-in closet and heaved things around until she unearthed her suitcase. It was a huge relic her mother had found at some garage sale years ago. She dropped it on the bed and flicked the catches. "It's his idea, actually. I wanted to get an annulment, but he wouldn't listen."

"An annulment?" Mo asked.

"Well, it might affect his business." Cassie grimaced when she heard how lame that sounded. She pulled an armload of jeans from her dresser and carried them to the suitcase that lay flat and open, like a gaping maw, on her bed. "A lot of people knew about his engagement to Melissa, and how she ended things between them. He's going to look foolish enough as it is, running off and marrying someone else on what was supposed to be the day he and the Icicle tied the knot. He'd look even dumber if we split as soon as we got back to Dallas."

Both her friends just stared at her. She dumped the jeans in the suitcase, which swallowed them with room to spare, and tried to make what she was doing sound more reasonable. "A business reputation can be fragile. Some investors might lose confidence in Gideon over this." The looks on their faces told her she wasn't improving. Cassie gave up and went back to the dresser, opened her lingerie drawer, and pulled out a pile of colorful cotton, silk and nylon. The nightgown on top, a bright red wisp of silk, slithered to the floor. She bent to pick it up.

"Oh, no, you don't." Jaya slid in front of the dresser, slammed the drawer shut and barred Cassie from it with her body. "You are not going to pack until you start making sense, you hear? Even you wouldn't agree to move in with a man just to help him keep his reputation solid in business. And why did you say *annulled* instead of *divorced?*"

"It doesn't matter, since we aren't getting either one. At least, not right away." She tossed the nightgown over her shoulder. Since Jaya was standing in front of the dresser and Mo blocked the closet, and since Cassie didn't want to tell her friends about Gideon's one-year trial plan, she turned and headed for the bathroom.

The phone rang. "Get that, will you?" she called, and opened the battered metal tackle box that held her makeup. She could fit in her toothbrush and toothpaste, but not much else. "Damn," she muttered. She still had to pack her shampoo and conditioner and eye drops and hair spray and first aid cream and curling iron and blow drier and...she put her hand on her stomach. It felt jumpy and unhappy.

"If you're this nervous," Mo said from the doorway, "maybe you should rethink what you're doing."

"There 's so much to the *business* part of marriage," she said. She'd never before considered the amount of paperwork involved in getting married. "I'll have to cancel my utilities, change the name on my credit cards and with Social Security."

He nodded, crossing his arms on his chest and leaning against the door frame. "Then there's the post office. You'll need to leave a change of address there, cancel the newspaper and change your magazine subscriptions."

Cassie bit her lip. She hadn't even moved in with Gideon, and already she felt as if her life were being swallowed up in his. "It makes sense to move into his place, though," she told Mo—or maybe herself. "It's bound to be a lot bigger than mine."

"Bound to," he said agreeably.

"It's probably all black-and-white, though," she muttered. She did remember Gideon's fondness for those two noncolors from her one visit to another apartment of his eight years ago. She sighed and turned, catching a glimpse of herself in the mirror. The cherry red nightgown was still draped over her shoulder. Thoughtfully she pulled the bit of silk provocation down and looked at it.

This was one thing, she understood suddenly, that she wouldn't need. Not yet. She had to keep some part of herself separate while they both adjusted to this marriage. Maybe, she thought with the optimism that was part of her, it wouldn't have to be for long. Maybe she'd be able to get under his guard, get him to let down his walls quickly once she was actually living with him.

Yes, she needed time. She was desperately vulnerable to him. She needed him to be a bit vulnerable, too, before they made love again.

Or for the first time, as far as he was concerned.

"Hey, Cassie," Jaya called from the other room. "This guy on the phone wants to know if you want to buy some supplemental accident insurance."

"Too late," she called back, flicking the nightgown up over the shower curtain rod. "Fate can't possibly have another accident in store for me." Not after yesterday's head-on collision.

"It's not too late," Mo corrected her. "You don't have to do this, Cassie, if it isn't what you want."

She met his eyes and said softly, "Maybe it was too late years ago."

He held her gaze steadily for a long moment. "Okay," he said at last, laying his hand on her shoulder. "No more questions, no more pressure. But you know where to come if you need anything, don't you?"

Her eyes filled. She smiled and nodded.

"Oh, no," Jaya said as she joined them. "Are you two getting sentimental on me?"

"Cover your eyes," Mo said equably. "We're almost finished." He gave Cassie's shoulder a last squeeze. "Since you're determined to do this, I'll go get that overnight case you always borrow when you visit your mom. You can load some of this stuff in it." He turned and left.

"You could help me pack, too," Cassie pointed out to the friend who remained, and started pulling things out of the medicine cabinet. She paused, holding up an odd-looking pile of glued-together seashells that usually sat on the vanity. It somewhat resembled an angel with chunky, gold-tipped wings.

Jaya folded her arms in front of her flat chest. "Help you screw up? I don't think so." She noticed what Cassie held and snorted. "I still can't believe you bought that thing. Artists are supposed to have some sort of standards."

"Art," Cassie said loftily, turning the little statue over to inspect it from a different angle, "is about genuine feeling. This is as genuine a piece of cheap tourist kitsch as any I've seen." And the old woman who made and sold the statues had delighted Cassie.

Jaya might have been reading her mind. "That old woman knew a pigeon when she found one."

"She did, didn't she?" Cassie smiled, remembering the mixture of shrewdness and humor in eyes cradled in several decades' worth of wrinkles. But amusement drained out as she considered the present. Wistfully she said, "I can't quite see this in any place Gideon owns, can you?"

"Cassie." Jaya's narrow face was earnest and worried. "Think about what you're doing, here. Running off and marrying Gideon Wilde is one thing—an impulse, maybe a mistake, but nothing you can't fix. Moving in with a man who doesn't want your stuff cluttering up his place is something else entirely."

Cassie had to smile at Jaya's unique slant on what was important. "Living together tends to follow marriage. And...I did make promises."

"Is that why you're doing this?" Jaya demanded. "Because you said 'I do' when some preacher told you to?"

"Maybe," Cassie admitted. There were other reasons, like the friendship between her brother and Gideon. She didn't want to see either man lose that, but it would be especially hard on Gideon. Cassie wasn't sure he had any other friends. "Mostly, though," she admitted at last, "I'm doing it for me. Because I've got a chance at him now, and I'd be a fool to toss that aside just because I'm scared, wouldn't I?"

"Lord, I don't know." Jaya ran an impatient hand through her hair, making the spiky bangs stand up straight. "I don't—what's that? It sounds like a truck."

Oh, Lord. "The movers." Still carrying the little shell angel, Cassie hurried out of the bathroom and looked out one of the windows.

Sure enough, in the driveway below, a man with a droopy mustache and a cigar was climbing down from the passenger side of a big, orange moving van. Cassie watched, paralyzed, as the door on the driver's side swung open and a skinny man in a red shirt stepped down.

They were here. They were going to pack up her things and put them away somewhere. Her fingers dug into the edges of the shells hard enough to hurt, but she didn't notice as she looked wildly around the room. What should she take with her? What had to be left behind?

She felt Jaya's hand on her shoulder. "You want me to get rid of them?" her friend asked.

Cassie looked down at the awkward angel, biting her lip and thinking about Gideon's apartment. Not his current apartment. He'd been living at an address not quite as expensive, not quite as exclusive, when she'd humiliated herself so thoroughly on the night of her twentieth birthday. But she remembered very clearly the white carpet, silvery gray couches and black lacquered tables. Just like she remembered the pale blond hair of the woman who'd been in his apartment.

That hair, the subtle shade of ripened wheat, had been the only color in the room.

Of course. Cassie's panic fled as she realized what she needed to do. "Jaya," she said slowly, "do me a favor and go tell those guys I won't be needing them, okay? They can bill Gideon for an hour of their time or something.''

Jaya whooped. "I knew it," she said, her long legs taking her to the door in a twinkling. "I knew you were too smart to do this."

"That's right," Cassie said, moving briskly herself now that she'd decided. She stopped at the little breakfast bar where Mickey Mouse held the telephone receiver out. "There's simply no reason to make all these decisions today. I'm paid up until the end of the month, so I'll leave most of the furniture here for now. We don't need to pay a mover for the other stuff."

"Cassandra Danielle O'Grady." Jaya turned, one hand on the doorknob. "What are you talking about? You aren't still planning on moving, are you?"

"My name," she said as she dialed, "is now Cassandra Danielle O'Grady *Wilde*." And that was the key. As of last night, she was part of Gideon's life. Even if he'd changed his mind and didn't want her there. Even if he did try to put fences around their relationship with his stupid one-year-marriage idea. Even if he had an apartment full of grays and blacks with no color....

Especially because he lived without color. He needed Cassie, needed her and her paints and her tacky little shell angel, and she didn't need to put half of her life in storage in order to be with him. She had to believe that, or give up hope right now.

Cassie was simply no good at giving up. "I thought I'd see if Sam and Nugget could bring a truck and some muscles," she explained to Jaya, who glared at her from the doorway, as Cassie listened to the phone ringing at the other end. "I'm sure Mo will help, too. Even if I leave some of the furniture here, there will be a lot of lifting involved, and it'll go faster if—oh, hi, Sam. I have a favor to ask. But first...guess what I did yesterday?"

Four

At 5:20 Gideon started clearing off his desk. He put the rolled seismic section he'd been studying into the stand behind his desk and shut down the computer. After a brief hesitation he put his working disk in his desk drawer, which he locked. He wouldn't take any work with him today. Cassie was waiting.

When he reached for his coffee cup he noticed the framed photograph that had sat on his desk for the past six months, a token that had reassured him daily of how close he was to his goal. How close he'd *thought* he was. The painful bewilderment that had ridden him for the past five days, ever since Melissa's phone call, rose again to tighten his throat.

He couldn't very well keep the picture of his former fiancée on his desk now that he'd married another woman, could he? Gideon picked up the picture.

Six months ago, when he and Melissa had become engaged, her parents had given him this studio photograph of their daughter, framed in silver. He held it in his hands now, feeling the weight of that heavy frame, staring at the lovely, poised

woman in the pale blue Chanel suit who was supposed to have
become his wife.

Why hadn't she wanted him?

It should have been perfect. They never argued, and their
tastes were almost identical. They'd agreed on everything from
music to movies to where they would live and what kind of
house they would live in. Oh, they'd had a minor difference
over the wedding itself. They'd agreed that the sanctuary at
St. Luke's was the only possible place for the ceremony, but
St. Luke's was the most fashionable church in the city. The
sanctuary had been booked up on weekends for the next two
years. Gideon had put his foot down. No way was he waiting
more than six months, as Melissa had urged at first. In the
end, she'd agreed to a weekday ceremony. At least she had
told him she agreed. How could he be sure of anything now?
She'd also told him she wanted to marry him, and she hadn't
meant that.

Slowly Gideon opened the back of the frame and slid out
the glossy photo. He unlocked his desk, opened the bottom
drawer and pulled out a photo album.

The album had been cheap to start with—a dull green binder
with gilt trim stamped into the vinyl. Now, many years and
much handling later, it looked shabby and completely out of
place in the elegant office.

Gideon sat at his desk and opened the album.

The first page made him smile. It held two pictures. One
was a yellowed newspaper clipping of a fair-haired girl in a
cheerleader's costume, and the other was an ad for a shiny
black Mustang cut from a magazine. Typical, he thought, of
a teenage boy's dreams: a cheerleader and a hot car.

Not that Gideon ever consciously thought of the album as
his dream book. He would have been insulted if someone told
him he was a dreamer. Dreams were fuzzy, illogical. He set
goals—rational, attainable goals.

Gideon had started the album when he was fifteen. He'd
been an unusual teenager, driven and determined—determined
to fight his way out of the life his childhood had led him to

expect. Driven to make something of himself. He'd read an article about visualizing goals to make them more concrete and achievable. From that he'd gotten the idea of finding pictures that represented those goals and keeping them in an album.

Of those first two goals, he'd eventually had to give up on the cheerleader. Cindy Matheson had gone steady with the same guy all through high school, and eventually married him. But there had been other girls, other women and other goals.

As for the car—he'd owned a black Mustang before he'd graduated from college. It hadn't been new, but it had been shiny and hot. Now he drove a Porsche.

Gideon turned the pages of the album, passing pictures of graduates in caps and gowns, pictures of stereos and stock certificates. And houses. Over and over he'd cut out pictures of houses, different versions of the house he would own someday. A house that would be a real home.

Unlike his former fiancée, Gideon knew exactly what he wanted. Only a house, he thought, could become a real home. The apartment he lived in now was pleasant and attractive, but it wasn't *home*.

Gideon believed in using professionals whenever possible. He'd long ago come to understand that he could not achieve his most important goal on his own. He couldn't make for himself the home he'd never had. It would be like expecting a deaf man to learn how to speak without the help of a hearing person. No, he'd realized he would have to turn over the business of making a home to someone trained for the job, one of that increasingly rare breed—the professional homemaker.

He soon realized it was just as well he'd already decided on wealth as a goal. The members of society who still consistently trained their daughters to be homemakers were the rich.

Gideon reached a blank page in the album and slid Melissa's photo inside the plastic sleeve.

Melissa had seemed perfect, he thought as he studied the elegant blonde. She was wealthy without being impossibly

rich, a quiet, coolly intelligent woman who lacked any distracting personal ambition to sidetrack her from the business
of making him a home. Gideon was aware that Melissa had
also been his aunt's choice for him, but he saw nothing in that
to disqualify her.

Why hadn't she wanted him?

He knew the fault lay with him. If only she'd explained,
given him something more specific, more useful, than one
teary phone call four nights before the wedding. He was
smothering her, she'd said. She couldn't live like this, she'd
said. She had to find out who she was, and her parents were
just going to have to accept that. Not that he would understand, she'd said, since he was always so sure of himself. He'd
never be able to understand.

She'd been right about that. He didn't understand at all.

Gideon put the album up and turned the key that locked his
desk. He stood, pausing to stare out the big window at the
traffic that crawled along the ribboned streets twenty-four
floors below. He seldom left this early. Downtown Dallas was
impressive to look at, convenient to work in, but the traffic at
quitting time could be hellish.

He had a wife waiting for him. The wrong wife. Everything
about Cassie was wrong. She was too hasty and emotional.
He'd always been comfortable around Melissa, but Cassie kept
him stirred up. Cassie was a mystery to him, too, and how
could you form a close relationship with someone you didn't
understand? Her warm, impulsive nature and peculiar version
of logic were exciting, he admitted, but so were chili peppers.
Neither one would suit him as a staple diet.

Beside, she was deeply involved with her own career, which
definitely wasn't homemaking. Still, he couldn't help the sexual rush he felt at the thought of Cassie waiting at his apartment for him. As far as Gideon was concerned, this would be
their real wedding night. He intended to make sure that after
tonight Cassie remembered last night as little as he did.

He wouldn't be drunk this time. He wouldn't lose control.
When he closed his office door behind him, the short hall

on the other side of the reception area was dark, indicating the rest of his staff had already left. He wasn't surprised to see his secretary still at her desk, though. He stopped to scowl at the woman pecking away at her keyboard. "You were supposed to leave twenty minutes ago. Don't try hitting me up for overtime when I specifically told you to go home."

Mrs. Pittinger had worked for Gideon ever since he'd struck out on his own. Her leathery face had more lines than a contour map, and her hair was a frazzled mess of shades of gray and bleached blond. Her bustline reminded Gideon of the prow of an aircraft carrier, and he often marveled at the engineering feat that kept everything firmly up and out. She was rude, loyal and brutally honest about everything except her age.

She was also a lousy typist. "Shut up, Wilde," she growled. "You'd better quit playing around with your pretty maps and get me another clerk, or you're going to owe me a fortune in overtime. A fortune," she repeated with satisfaction, hitting the Save button. "And I will collect."

"Leech," he muttered. "If you don't have a clerk it's your own fault. You've driven off every one I've hired for you."

"Ha! It was you who scared off that last one."

Since she was right, Gideon declined to argue. Instead he looked at the long, white florist's box on the credenza behind Mrs. Pittinger. "Good. They got here in time." He frowned. "That doesn't look like two dozen."

"I only ordered one dozen." The printer burst into action as Mrs. Pittinger rolled her chair back. "I told you—a dozen roses tonight, two dozen in a month for your anniversary." She stood. "I got you some champagne, too."

Gideon felt a familiar irritation. Not that the failure to follow orders surprised him. He'd long ago given up trying to get respectful obedience out of his secretary. What never failed to aggravate him, though, was how often she was right. "Thanks," he said curtly.

She bent to retrieve her purse. "Don't fall all over yourself with gratitude."

He reached into his back pocket for his wallet. "What do I owe you for the champagne?"

She muttered something unintelligible, her chin down as she dug around in the suitcase-size purse.

"How much?"

She aimed a frown at him. "I said that it's on me. Congratulations."

He felt foolishly pleased. "Thanks," he said again. The corner of his mouth tugged up in spite of him.

Mrs. Pittinger hadn't said much when he'd called her into his office that afternoon and told her he wanted two dozen roses to take home to his new wife, and to please send a notice of the marriage to the *Morning News*. She'd looked at him suspiciously, then said, "I thought that blond Barbie doll of yours dumped you."

"I married Ryan O'Grady's sister, Cassie," he'd told her stiffly, "not Melissa."

He'd managed, at least, to surprise her. "The artist? Well," she'd muttered, "we'll see."

Gideon looked at his secretary now and wondered if the champagne was a gesture of congratulations, or of sympathy. "I suppose you spread the word around here." No one had bearded him in his office to offer congratulations, but he would have been enormously surprised if they had. His employees understood that when his door was closed he wasn't to be interrupted for anything short of the Second Coming—except, of course, for Mrs. Pittinger. She interrupted when and how she chose.

"I told them." She looked pleased, in a gloomy sort of way, and shoved the letter the printer had finished at him. "Here, sign this before you go. Vicky wants to give you a wedding shower."

He stared at her blankly.

She gave a bark of laughter. "That was my thought. Foster wants to go over your changed tax situation as a married man, and Pete wishes he had the nerve to ask if you got a prenuptial agreement. Janis asked all kinds of questions that were none of her business, and Ed looked like a fish when he heard. Just stood there mouth-breathing and didn't say a word.''

Gideon grimaced and grabbed the florist's box and the champagne. ''I'm glad I was able to provide my staff with a few minute's entertainment.''

''You've never done anything half so amusing,'' his secretary agreed. She fell into step with him when he locked the office door and strode down the elegantly appointed hallway to the elevator.

He punched the Down button twice, as if that would make a difference.

''In a hurry, Wilde?''

''No,'' he said, and barely kept himself from punching the button a third time. ''The traffic will be bad at this time of day.''

She gave that bark of laughter again. ''And you don't want whatever your new bride has cooked up for you to get cold, do you?''

''Cassie does cook,'' he said, choosing to take her comment at face value. ''Ryan has bragged about her cooking lots of times.'' It occurred to Gideon that Cassie might have supper waiting when he got there. The idea pleased him.

''I don't know.'' Mrs. Pittinger shook her head dubiously. The elevator dinged and opened. ''My second husband was a sculptor,'' she announced, stepping in. ''Charming people, artists. Passionate. But hardly domestic.''

He followed, bemused. Mrs. Pittinger and passion? ''I didn't know you'd been married twice,'' he said, somewhat at a loss, as the elevator door closed behind them.

''Three times,'' she said, and looked smug. ''I like men.''

This new image of the secretary who'd bullied him for the past nine years kept Gideon silent all the way down. The elevator filled long before they reached the ground floor, and he and Mrs. Pittinger were carried off in opposite directions by the tide of quitting workers in the lobby. But he was smiling as he unlocked his Porsche in the underground parking area.

So Mrs. Pittinger liked men, did she? Well, he'd had indications that his new bride liked men just fine, too. At least she liked one man—her husband. Which was how it should be.

Life is seldom what it should be.

Gideon had clues before he parked his car in the covered parking at his apartment complex. The Chevy four-by-four occupying his parking space was a hint, as were the two young men wrestling with an ugly, paint-spattered table in the bed of that pickup. One wore a shirt. The other didn't. Neither looked like a professional mover. His next clue was the muscular fellow he rode up with in the elevator. This one had dreadlocks and a packing box full of books.

By the time Gideon stepped out of the elevator, florist's box under one arm, champagne in the other hand, and saw that his front door stood wide open to let the hard rock sound of the Foo Fighters entertain his neighbors, he was pretty sure he wouldn't find any supper simmering on the stove.

He wasn't prepared for what he did find.

The number of boxes camped out on his living room floor weren't a surprise. By the time he reached his door, he was expecting them. The sheer amount of the debris spread across both leather couches and spilling onto the ivory wool of the area rug was a bit of a shock, though.

A pile of clothing covered the end of one couch in multicolored disarray, dripping hangers onto the floor. A bright yellow ceramic lamp with a dented shade tottered at the other end, with the space between covered in sheets, towels, and a magnificent Navajo blanket. A slow cooker balanced precariously on top of the linens, with a handful of silk daisies tucked under the lid.

The other couch was just as full, though its contents were a mix of his own familiar possessions, such as the set of encyclopedias he kept in the guest room, and her odd…stuff. Some of it was so odd he had no idea what it was, like the tacky little whatsit made of seashells. But the mess on and around the couches was not enough by itself to crack the lid on his temper.

The furniture came close. Not Cassie's furniture. His. Everything from the two guest rooms was jammed up together in his normally spacious living room. A box spring and mattress reclined against one wall, while a floor lamp arched over a towering pile of bureau drawers. At the moment he couldn't spot the chest the drawers belonged to, but that may have been because of the empty armoire, its doors hanging open, that blocked his view of the dining area.

But the careless disposal of his things wasn't really what started the knot of anger twisting in his stomach. Cassie did.

Her back was to him. So was that of the young man on whose shoulders she sat, jigging slightly to the beat of the deafening music. She was hanging some sort of peculiar woven thing with feathers and twigs on the wall facing the entry. The rug-size creation hung nearly to the floor, even with her extra elevation...on another man's shoulders.

Her mount stepped sideways.

Cassie's round little bottom, lovingly revealed by her worn jeans, swayed with their movement. Her legs hugged that other man's chest, and his hands clasped her calves. His blond head looked pale and bright against the indigo denim of her jeans and the dark green of her T-shirt. He had a big nose and big teeth, and he was laughing.

Gideon couldn't name what he felt, couldn't understand the violence of the storm sleeting through him. It was too new. Too strong. Instinctively he retreated to the iciest part of the storm, away from the heat and lightning at its center.

He didn't speak. He wasn't sure enough of his control—or that he could be heard over the din. He strode to the stereo, shifted flowers and champagne to one arm and, with a yank, pulled the plug.

The sudden silence was broken immediately "Hey, Cassie-girl," called out the young man with the dreadlocks who'd entered, unseen, behind Gideon. "I changed my mind. I'll take that lamp for my help, after all, instead of your sweet body. I don't think this fellow would appreciate my first choice."

Cassie wondered why Nugget had shut off the music. She

didn't pay much attention to what he said. Nugget was apt to say anything. She twisted her head to look, but Mo turned at the same time, putting a bit of a wobble into her position. Since the wall hanging seemed to be straight at last, she abandoned it and grabbed Mo's head. "I keep telling you the lamp's a better bargain, Nugget. I—oh." A flash of mingled heat and nerves hit Cassie the moment she saw Gideon. "Hi."

He didn't look happy. Gorgeous, yes. Why would a woman who'd always thought men looked best in faded jeans feel a sharp sexual tug at the sight of a grim-faced man in a custom-tailored suit? Maybe it was knowing what those wide shoulders looked like without the suit...and having some dim, rapidly receding memory of what that hard face looked like when he smiled.

She sighed. "I'm sorry about the mess," she said, tapping on Mo's head. "C'mon, Mo, set me down." Her friend carried her to one of the couches, muttering about how he'd known this wasn't a good idea, and she'd darn well better be ready to pay his medical bills.

"I'm not that heavy," she said absently, her attention on the silent man watching her. "I thought we'd be done before now," she told Gideon apologetically, slipping from Mo's shoulders to the back of the couch and from there to the floor. "But we had to move a lot of stuff around to make room for my things."

"So I see." Deliberately, as if the action required great precision, he set the bottle and the long, white box he carried on the big, square coffee table. "Did the moving company fail to show up?" he asked politely. "If you had let me know, I would have taken care of it."

"No, they came." She bit her lip. She was not fooled by the smooth glaze of courtesy into thinking he was taking this well. "I had Jaya send them away. I don't think you've met Jaya..." She looked around, vaguely aware that she hadn't seen her friend for a while.

"She left for the club an hour ago," Mo said drily. "It's six-thirty."

"Oh. Well." Cassie spread her hands and tried a smile. "We've been really busy, though it may not look like it, with all this mess. But I, ah, changed my mind about putting my things in storage. I left the couch and some stuff back at the apartment—the rent's paid up, after all—but it just somehow seemed easier to bring most of it over here and sort of see what fits."

"I see. You are certainly entitled to keep your possessions, rather than storing them. I wish you had discussed it with me, however."

The temperature in the room kept going down. Her chin came up. "The way we discussed it earlier, when you told me what to do?"

"You didn't object."

She absolutely hated it when he was logical. "I should have called you," she admitted grudgingly.

Nugget interrupted to say that he'd better be going. Cassie flushed, embarrassed that she'd forgotten to introduce her friends. She did so, and Gideon managed to be terribly polite and insulting at the same time. She wanted to hit him. Nugget told Gideon he was a lucky man and repeated that he really did need to be going. Mo asked her quietly if she wanted him to hang around—as if he thought she might be afraid of Gideon.

He must not have been quiet enough. Gideon's gaze fixed on him, sharp as the edge of a sabre. God knows what anyone would have said or done next, but fortunately her table arrived on the backs of Sam and Arturo. Tension dissipated in comic relief when the two men and a table tried to get through the door and couldn't.

Fifteen minutes later the table was in the room Cassie had claimed for her studio, her friends were on their way out of the building, and Gideon stood at the bar that angled between the dining and living areas. He'd taken off his suit jacket and unbuttoned the top two buttons of his shirt before grabbing one end of the table and organizing its arrival in her studio.

Cassie remembered what his chest and back looked like,

and part of her wished he'd gone ahead and taken the shirt off, too. Although she shouldn't wish for such a thing. They were about to have a fight, and she found him distracting enough in crisp white cotton. Bare skin would have put her at a definite disadvantage.

"All right." Cassie stood in the center of the chaotic living room, her hands on her hips. "They're gone, so now you can tell me what an inconsiderate idiot I was. I should have called you when I changed my mind. I know I should have, but this 'being married' business is new to me."

"Obviously." He poured a single shot of Scotch over the ice in his glass.

Her eyes narrowed. There was a bite in his voice that had been absent before, and his beautiful mouth was thin with anger. "What does that mean?"

"I don't care to argue, Cassie." He nodded at the white box. "You'd better open that. They'll need to go in water."

She wanted him to argue, dammit. A good argument would wipe that remote expression off his face. But—she turned her head—she also wanted to know what was in that box. Something that needed to go in water? Probably not goldfish, she thought as she took one step, then another, toward the coffee table.

"Oh!" She stood, the lid in one hand, and smiled helplessly at the long-stemmed roses, so richly red it seemed the color would drip right off them. "Oh, they're beautiful." She bent and scooped them carefully out of the box. "I could mix colors forever and not get a red this deep, and the smell..." Somewhere, she thought, inhaling the dizzying perfume, somewhere she had that vase a potter friend had given her. Its blue-white glaze would be stunning with these red, red roses.

She turned, her smile soft with the pleasure he'd given her. "This is the second time you've given me flowers."

"Is it? I don't recall the other occasion, I'm afraid."

The look of disinterest on his face was like a slap. "Yesterday. At our wedding. My bouquet." Which she'd saved and now rested on the bottom shelf of the refrigerator. "But, of course, you wouldn't remember that, would you?"

He sipped his drink, studying her over the rim of his glass. "I'm sure Mrs. Pittinger will be pleased to hear that the florist she uses deserves our business."

"Mrs. Pittinger?" Balanced tightly between extremes of anger and hurt, Cassie bent to set the roses back in their box as carefully as Gideon had put the box down half an hour ago.

"My secretary. I'll have to introduce you." He set his drink, unfinished, down on the bar. "Perhaps it was just as well that I walked in on the...confusion here today. It points up the fact that we really haven't discussed what we each expect from this marriage. A year is a long time to live together. It's best that we understand each other." He started toward her. "Although I believe I have some idea of your needs, financially and...otherwise."

Her hands went to her hips. "You obviously know nothing about what I need."

"Oh, I think I do. You needn't worry, Cassie. I'm not unreasonable. I like your physical, demonstrative nature, and I'm not unfair enough to hold anything you've done in the past against you."

"Well, that's damned big of you!"

"But the present," he went on, stopping a foot and a half from her, "the present is different. Whatever your habits may have been before, you are my wife now and I will not tolerate the kind of spectacle I saw today."

She was used to the tangy spice of anger. This feeling was different—raw, unstable, overwhelming. "Spectacle?" Her voice rose. "Just what do you mean by that?"

"I mean the sight you treated me to of my new bride riding another man with his head between your legs."

Shock drained the blood from her face. For one long, stupid moment she simply could not believe he had said what she'd heard him say. Then she spun around and started moving away from him. Anywhere, as long as it was away.

She might have escaped if she hadn't stumbled over an

empty box. His hand shot out and stopped her. "Dammit, Cassie, is this your answer to anything that upsets you? To run away?"

She jerked her arm free and faced him, nearly panting with hurt and anger. "Leave me alone."

"Not," he said implacably, "until you understand and agree to my terms."

"Terms? If you mean that you don't intend for me to have friends of the opposite sex, you can go—"

"I mean that I will not allow you to have lovers while we're married."

"Fine!" she shouted, and, putting both hands on his chest, shoved as hard as she could. He looked greatly surprised as he fell back a step. "Excellent!" she yelled as she followed him. "Abso-damn-lutely great idea! I won't have any lovers while we're married, and that—" she shoved again "—includes—" another shove "—you!"

She had five whole seconds to watch his expression change while her own anger drained out, as it always did, quickly and completely, leaving a shaky feeling behind. Not fear, she told herself. She wasn't afraid of Gideon. She took a deep breath. "This isn't quite the way I'd planned to broach the subject," she began in her most reasonable tone of voice.

His expression was unreadable, but it definitely wasn't cold when he stepped toward her.

Instinctively, she retreated. "Really, Gideon, it's perfectly logical for us to get to know each other better before we, ah, become intimate."

"We've known each other for sixteen years." He advanced.

It was silly to feel like he was stalking her. Silly...yet she moved to put the coffee table between them. "Yes, well, maybe one of us hasn't been paying very good attention for those sixteen years. You still think I married you for your money, don't you? As for what you thought about me just now..." That hurt was too raw to speak of. She wasn't about to excuse herself by explaining Mo's sexual preferences, either, dammit. She shouldn't have to.

He came around the table. "I'm paying attention now," he said softly, and it sounded more like a threat than a promise. "And there's a lot I intend to learn about you, Cassie."

She edged around the couch, fascinated by the contrast between the storms building in his eyes and the tightness at his mouth that spoke of grim control. Which would win—the storms, or his control? A shiver traveled over her that had nothing to do with cold and everything to do with the edgy feeling strumming through her. "Gideon?"

He started around the couch.

"Good grief, Gideon, quit this. You're making me nervous."

"Good."

"You're acting very strange." Maybe nervous wasn't the right word for what she felt. Restless? Prickly, as if some subtle electric charge had every cell of her body standing at attention. "If you're worried that I've embarrassed you, you needn't be. I was discreet about my decision. That's one reason my clothes are all over the place, because I didn't want to put them away in the back bedroom before my friends left. I thought you'd probably rather they didn't know I wasn't moving into your bedroom."

"Thank you," he said acidly. "That was considerate. Unnecessary, but considerate."

He was on the same side of the couch as she was. Too close. "I'm not moving into your bedroom," she told him, and stepped back.

She wasn't prepared. After his slow stalk, she wasn't expecting him to move so fast. His hands on her arms yanked her up against him. She wasn't prepared for how fast heat could hit, either. Like an earthquake, it shuddered through her, making her senses reel even as she staggered, her balance lost, amazed by the thrill of being off balance, caught and held.

"You're my wife," he said harshly, a scary, beautiful blaze burning in his dark eyes. "However the marriage started, however badly I failed you last night, you are my wife and you will sleep in my bed. When I allow you to sleep…" His hands slid up her arms to her shoulders, her neck, where they lingered erotically, his fingers skimming her throat.

"There's no such thing as a temporary wife," she whispered as chills chased each other over her goose-pimpled flesh. She had never thought of intimacy as submission, but she desperately wanted to submit now, to let him do whatever he wanted...but she couldn't. "Don't make love to me, Gideon, unless you're ready to give up your one-year trial plan."

"No conditions," he growled, and he threaded his fingers in her hair and pulled, tilting her head back. "What's between us has nothing to do with rules, and everything to do with...this." His head came down.

Heat. Crisp enough on the edges to slice a woman open. Power. It shot through her as fast as the heat when his mouth took hers. His power—hers—she couldn't tell, knew only that it sang through her veins like liquor. He didn't pause to woo, or wait on her invitation to deepen the kiss. His thumb pressed her jaw to make her mouth open for him, and his tongue swept in. She moaned, tasting Gideon, tasting a freedom as rich and exciting as the stomach-clenching roll of a roller coaster ride. There was fear in this ride, but so much more.

Gideon was lost. From the moment his lips crushed down on hers, he was lost. He knew it and didn't care, knew, too, that he should stop before he raised hopes in her he had no intention of fulfilling. But he didn't care, couldn't care, not with her body hot, electrically alive in his arms. Her mouth was as avid as his. When she moaned, he pulled her impossibly closer, kneading the fullness of her bottom with one hand while his other slid under her shirt to seek her breast. He raced for an edge he'd never known existed, a limit so much a part of him it had never occurred to him to challenge it. Until now.

He nearly went over that edge. Her scent, her eagerness, the feel of her small breast and hard nipple in his palm—those were almost enough on their own to topple him. But needs battered him. *His.* He had to make her his. Now. Quickly. He had to be inside her, had to—

He had her jeans unsnapped before he knew he was going

to strip her. If she hadn't tried to help, her hand colliding awkwardly with his at her zipper, he would have taken her there on the crowded floor of the living room. But that one second's distraction, that tiny pause, let him hear the voice at the back of his mind. The one he didn't know came from fear.

I can't lose control. I won't. I won't be like my father.

It was enough.

His hands went from her pants to her arms. He inhaled once, raggedly, his head bent to pull her scent into him. Then he put her from him.

Maybe if she hadn't stared at him with such innocent bewilderment—if her mouth hadn't been so swollen, and her eyes so slumberously inviting, in spite of the dawning confusion—maybe he could have been reasonable. Maybe he could have explained, slowed things down, kept himself from taking her like a beast.

But not when she reached out for him with one pale hand. The one wearing his ring.

Gideon did the only thing he could do. He left without a word.

Five

At 12:23 Cassie stopped waiting for Gideon to come home. She'd unpacked the boxes from her kitchen and put away her clothes in an effort to distract herself while she waited. Now she lay in her old bed in its new place in Gideon's guest room and stared up at the darkness.

She wanted to be angry. Anger made sense, under the circumstances. He shouldn't have kissed her that way. He certainly had no business kissing her that way and then going away for hours. And she *could* have gotten angry. If only she could have forgotten the look in his eyes when he pulled away from her, the certainty that however strongly his rejection cut her, he was bleeding from a worse wound, she felt sure she could have worked up a good fit of temper.

At least, she told herself, she knew her kiss had affected him. This time he wouldn't forget that he'd kissed her.

She rolled onto her side and punched the pillow into a new position. The clock on the bedside table—her clock, her table, from what used to be her apartment—said 1:03. She wasn't one blink closer to sleep than when she lay down forty minutes ago.

Had it been a mistake to move her things into this room? She'd wanted the comfort of having familiar objects around her. But maybe, she conceded in the lonely dark, if she added her decision to surround herself with her possessions to her determination to stay out of Gideon's bed, she could understand it if he thought she was a roommate, not a wife.

If she was his roommate, she had no claim on him. Which meant he might be anywhere right now. With anyone.

She huffed her breath out impatiently and rolled onto her back. Gideon was stubborn, arrogant and endlessly honest. If she wanted to know whether he considered himself bound by the vows he barely remembered making, she just had to ask him.

Cassie pulled the covers up under her chin and tried not to think of blondes.

Six months ago, Cassie had gone to Gideon's engagement party with her brother. It had seemed like a good idea, a way to put her stupid dreams to rest once and for all. So she knew what Melissa looked like. The Icicle was a blonde. She spoke in a low, pleasant voice and wore boring, beautiful clothes. The only thing ostentatious about the woman was her breasts. Not, Cassie admitted reluctantly, that they were really cow-sized breasts. Just…large. About the size of grapefruits, maybe.

Grapefruits. She sniffed. All Cassie had was apples. Granny Smith apples, at that.

She grinned suddenly, unable to hang on to the self-pity. Lots of people like apples better than grapefruit, after all.

She tossed the covers back and stood up. She wasn't going to sleep anytime soon. She had to either paint or eat—and since she hadn't gotten her studio set up yet, it must be time to raid the refrigerator.

The kitchen was a cook's dream, with a black-and-white tile floor, spotless white cabinets, and shiny black countertops. The refrigerator was a big, black side-by-side that held milk, the contents of Cassie's old refrigerator, her wedding bouquet, and the pizza she'd ordered after Gideon left. The pantry was bigger than the bathroom in her old apartment. Until Cassie had unpacked the boxes from her kitchen, though, that marvelous pantry had been bare except for paper towels and canned chili, which Gideon apparently bought in bulk, and three boxes of cereal.

Two of those boxes, she remembered, smiling as she pulled the pizza box from the refrigerator, contained healthy, multigrain brands. They were nearly full. The third cereal was one of those godawful sugar-packed diet-killers that mothers try to keep their kids from eating. It had been almost empty.

So Gideon liked something sweet in the mornings, did he? Waffles, she decided, tapping her foot as she waited for the microwave to ding. She ought to make him eat cold pizza for breakfast, but he'd be expecting that sort of treatment, wouldn't he? Instead she'd make him whole wheat waffles.

He would be here for breakfast. She was sure of it. Where could he go? Not to Ryan, certainly. Not to Melissa. Besides, tomorrow—today, rather—was Thursday. Gideon wouldn't miss work, and he wouldn't go to the office without coming home long enough to shower and change, no matter how upset he was.

Just how upset was he? And why had kissing her sent him running?

The smell of hot cheese, spices, and pepperoni made her stomach growl when she pulled the pizza out of the microwave. She put the big slice on a folded paper towel and blew on it as she wandered back into the living room.

She settled on the thick carpet in front of the wall-size window without turning on any more lights. It was really a beautiful apartment...if you liked blacks and grays. The view was great. She was five stories up, high enough to turn the city's lights into a collage with some of the glowing beads moving, others still. Just high enough, she thought, to feel detached from what she saw. That would appeal to Gideon.

Maybe Gideon's need for detachment was why he was gone
now. He'd been anything but detached when he'd kissed her.

She ate carefully, not wanting to stain the ivory carpet. On
the whole, she was pleased with what she'd done with the
apartment so far, though she still had to find places for a lot
of things. But she'd added some color. She'd put up a couple
of her paintings, an abstract she particularly liked and a
slightly surreal painting of a red horse charging through bil-
lows of yellow dust. The woven sculpture Mo had helped her
hang was perfect. Its turquoise and rusty red were repeated in
the Navajo blanket she'd slung across the back of one of the
buttery-soft leather couches.

Those couches. She frowned at them, irritated. Gideon had
plenty of money. You'd think he would have replaced them
by now. She shouldn't have to sit here and look at them and
remember....

It had been raining. The second day of January usually
meant bad weather, so Cassie often celebrated her birthday
under leaden skies, with snow, rain or ice as a sort of heavenly
confetti. She remembered the car she'd driven to Gideon's
apartment—an old bug she'd named Beetle Bailey after the
lazy soldier in the funnies. The transmission had been giving
her trouble. She'd driven all the way to Garland without using
any of the freeways that laced Dallas to its suburbs, because
Bailey had refused to shift into fourth.

Gideon had been surprised when he'd opened his door and
seen her. Oh, yes, she thought, nodding grimly to herself in
the darkened living room, she had managed to surprise the
man. Some might say she'd shocked the hell out of him.

If only she hadn't been so obvious. But Cassie didn't have
much subtlety now. At twenty she'd been as subtle as a blow-
torch. Her dress had been red, of course, and tight. Very tight.

At least, in the process of throwing herself at him, she
hadn't blurted out how much she loved him. Cassie hoped, as
she'd been hoping for the past eight years, that Gideon had
put her behavior down to an advanced case of lust brought on
by rioting hormones.

Cassie sighed and, with all the distaste and determination of a housewife getting to that grimy spot behind the refrigerator, she remembered the blonde.

It hadn't occurred to Cassie that she and Gideon weren't alone. One of those blasted couches had sat with its back to the door, so she hadn't known about the blonde until the woman sat up, crossed her arms on the couch's back, and smiled.

Long, silvery blond hair. That had been the first thing Cassie had noticed about the woman, other than the dreadful fact of her presence in Gideon's apartment while Cassie stood, her arms twined around Gideon's neck, his hands on her shoulders keeping her from pressing herself fully against him. Then she'd noticed that the woman's arms and shoulders were bare.

And she'd seen the black lace bra tossed over the back of the couch.

Cassie didn't remember exactly what the woman had said, mainly because she'd spent too much time in the months afterward rewriting the scenario and giving herself better lines. It had been something amused, though, and tolerant. Quite horridly tolerant, because obviously she knew Cassie was no threat. Something like, "Who's your little friend, Gideon?"

Cassie glowered at the pale gray couches. Why did Gideon have to have a thing for blondes? It was so blasted predictable of him. Lots of men had a preference for blondes. Gideon needed to develop more individuality in his tastes.

He needs me, she told herself, rising to carry her greasy paper towel back to the kitchen. He definitely did not need the type of woman he always seemed to pick—cool, sophisticated, the sort who was too comfortable within her own walls to ever challenge his.

Sixty seconds later she lay down once more in her old bed in its new room and stared up at the darkened ceiling. At least, she told herself again, she knew her kiss had affected him. She wondered again about the oddly devastated look in his eyes right after he'd pushed her away. And she didn't sleep, couldn't keep her eyes closed long enough to fall asleep, until she heard the front door open and close.

He didn't turn any lights on. She knew it was Gideon, though, would have known it even if she hadn't heard the thud and his muffled oath when he walked into one of the pieces of furniture she'd moved around earlier.

She glanced at her clock. It was 2:05.

The master bedroom was on the opposite side of the apartment from the guest rooms, so she didn't actually hear him go to bed. But he was home.

She closed her eyes. By 2:11, she was asleep.

He knew she was up. Gideon had heard Cassie moving around when he first woke up the next morning, so he knew she was up. If he couldn't help wishing she'd go back to bed before he finished showering, he still knew it was better to get the inevitable over with.

Damn, but he hated apologizing.

He smelled the coffee as soon as he stepped out of his room. He had his tie slung around his neck and was adjusting the collar of his shirt when he reached the kitchen doorway. And stopped.

She wore a long-sleeved, blue-and-white-striped pajama shirt. No pants. Just the shirt. It hit her a little above mid-thigh.

How could anyone that small have such long legs?

"Ready in a minute."

"Hmm?" He dragged his attention up to her face. Her smiling face. Why was she smiling at him instead of throwing things? Did she know he'd woken up hard as a board this morning, and that the sight of her in that shirt was pure punishment when he couldn't touch her?

Was she wearing panties?

"I said that you can have the first batch of waffles. Here, sit down." She gestured at one of the two old kitchen chairs he hadn't let the decorator get rid of.

He moved to the coffeepot instead of following Cassie's instructions.

She bustled over to the pantry, calling over her shoulder, "Refill my cup while you're at it, would you? It's by the stove." She emerged with two place mats. He'd never seen them before. They had ruffles and they didn't match. "You're not a morning person, are you?" she asked as she set the mismatched place mats on his table, which, he noticed, also held a glass bud vase that wasn't his.

One of the roses he'd brought her yesterday was in the vase.

"I've always gotten up early." Irritated for no reason that he could think of, he put his coffee on the solid blue place mat, set hers on the one with yellow sunflowers and sat down. "You're making waffles?"

"Mmm-hmm. Ordinarily I'd offer you some of this really great fruit compote I make—it's much better for you than syrup—but I—" The microwave dinged. "Is maple syrup okay?"

Speechless, he nodded while she took a small pitcher with hot syrup from the microwave and set it on the table beside him. While she hurried around, putting whipped butter and orange juice on the table, he looked at her legs and wondered what the hell was going on.

She set a white pottery plate holding two golden waffles in front of him. They smelled wonderful. He couldn't help thinking about how close this was to the fantasy he'd indulged in yesterday about her in his kitchen, cooking for him. Except that he hadn't pictured her legs so thoroughly bare.

Reality could actually improve on fantasy, he decided. In a miserably frustrated sort of way.

"Plate's hot," she told him cheerfully. Then she sat down across from him, picked up the folded newspaper by her chair in one hand, her coffee cup in the other and forgot his existence.

"Where's your meal?" he demanded, spreading the butter on thickly.

"Cooking. You have to get to work, so you can have the

first batch." She put the paper down and smiled. "This isn't a precedent, you know. I'm not going to fix you waffles every morning."

"I don't usually eat much breakfast." The scent of hot maple syrup mingled with that of melted butter and the waffles themselves, yet he didn't take a bite.

"Just cereal, right?"

"Right." He looked at the hot, luscious waffles for a moment longer. "I guess I'm wondering if you put a little extra something in mine. Something to pay me back for the way I acted last night."

She spoke very dryly. "Live dangerously. Dig in."

Unable to resist, he did.

Half of the newspaper, including the business section, sat by his place. Since she turned her attention back to her portion of the paper, he felt no qualms about reading while he ate. It wasn't until he was mopping up the last of the syrup with the last bite of waffle that he realized what section of the paper she was studying.

He frowned. "What are you doing with the Help Wanted ads?"

"Oh," she said, pausing to circle something, "when I called Ryan this morning, he fired me." She glanced up, saw his expression and grinned. "Well, the job was never anything but a compromise between Ryan's need to take care of me and my need to take care of myself. When my last employer went belly-up and I couldn't find something right away, Ryan insisted he needed his phone answered and his filing done. Really, though, my brother and I do not belong in the same office day after day."

He reached across the table and pulled the paper out of her hands.

"Hey!"

"I can't believe it." He looked at the items she'd circled. "Sales Clerk Wanted." "Waitress Wanted." Several more along the same lines. "You actually intend to apply for these?" She wasn't *supposed* to work, dammit, except at her painting. That was their deal. She was supposed to stay here, in his apartment, where he had put her. And paint.

"Hey, I'm a pretty good waitress. It's in the blood. If you're wondering about my degree, maybe you've forgotten that it's in art. You add that to my work history and—"

"You are not going to work."

Both her eyebrows went up. "I beg your pardon."

"I spoke clearly enough."

"I pay my own way," she said levelly. "I always have."

"You are not going to work at some two-bit job out of some misguided sense of pride. You are my wife, and I—"

"Misguided?" Her eyes narrowed and her voice rose. "Misguided?"

"For God's sake, Cassie, you married me so you wouldn't have to do this!" He waved the folded newspaper. It rustled emphatically. "Whatever quixotic notion you have about proving you don't need my money, you can just forget it."

She stood, spread her hands flat on the table, leaned forward and scowled in his face. "Are you telling me you're such a chauvinistic moron that you don't think women should work?"

"Of course not. But there's a difference between this sort of job and a real career, for God's sake."

She made a strangled sound and straightened. To his horror, her eyes grew damp.

"Cassie." He stood quickly, appalled. "Don't cry. I'm a jerk. Just don't cry."

"I'm not crying!" she yelled, wiping the moisture from her eyes. "I'm mad! And oh, I hate it when I get s-so mad I cry, and then I can't argue right and just sound stupid." She paused to glare at him through shiny-damp eyes, her hands fisted at her sides. "This is *not* some pathetic female ploy."

He wanted to grin. God, how he wanted to grin—in amusement and with a crazy, unreasonable relief. Why would he be relieved by her anger? His emotions kept swinging wildly this morning, reinforcing what he'd learned last night: she was dangerous to him.

And all he could think of now, looking at her eyes bright with feeling, her beautifully naked legs, and the two small bumps her breasts made beneath that wrinkled pajama shirt, was that she really was gorgeous when she was mad. It took every bit of control he could muster not to point that out to her. "There's nothing really wrong with those other jobs," he said diplomatically. "But your career is art, which makes those jobs wrong for you. That's all I meant."

Her eyes stayed narrowed for a long moment. Then her lip twitched. "It is, huh?" As quick as that, her anger was gone. She chuckled. "I don't believe it for a minute, you know, but you get points for trying." Then she reached across the table for the paper.

He watched her smooth out the paper and go right back to studying the Help Wanted columns. She really was going to do this, he realized. She was going to go out and work at some job she didn't want, didn't need, instead of working at her art. "There's a job opening at my office," he heard himself say.

She looked up. "That's sweet of you, Gideon, but I want a real job."

"This would be real enough," he said dryly, "but it might be temporary. Every so often I hire a clerk to help my secretary. I believe the score stands at Mrs. Pittinger four, clerks zero. The longest any of them lasted was about two months."

Cassie's mouth twitched. "So you wouldn't be doing me any favors?"

"Nope." Had he lost his mind? Anyone would think he *wanted* to have her around, when the opposite was true. He wanted her, all right, but she came with a price attached. A price he couldn't afford.

He'd wanted to believe differently. In spite of the vicious jealousy he'd experienced when he'd seen her with that "friend" of hers, Gideon had wanted to think of Cassie as—well, not promiscuous. Cassie could never cheapen herself. But she was warm, impulsive, physical—which could have added up to a woman who enjoyed the transitory burn of passion without getting tangled up in it. A woman he could have.

Temporarily.

Yet even after she warned him differently, he hadn't stopped until he realized the danger to himself, not just to her. He wasn't proud of himself this morning.

Cassie gave a nod. "Sure. I mean, why not? This is one time I won't have to feel guilty if the job doesn't work out. Your secretary's history as a boss is as bad as mine as an employee." She grinned. "You'll be glad to hear that I do have some oil and gas experience. I worked as a draftsman for nearly three months at a small exploration firm once."

Gideon had to get over his lust for this woman. She drew too much from him. Threatened too much. Yet now he knew how she smelled, how she tasted, how erotic she looked sitting at his kitchen table with a thoughtful expression on her face and nothing on the long, silky legs—legs that were bare nearly to her...he shifted uncomfortably in the hard, wooden chair.

"Good," he said, and wondered how he was going to explain to Mrs. Pittinger that he'd just hired her a clerk with an unfortunate habit of getting fired when she didn't quit, or have the whole company fold under her. "You can start as soon as you're settled in here." He glanced around. She'd almost finished putting her things away last night, while he was gone. Guilt bit deep. He'd done what he had to do, though. If he'd stayed, he wouldn't have given her the option of which bed to sleep in. "Start tomorrow, if you like. The job is part-time, from eight until noon." At least she'd still be able to paint in the afternoons this way.

"Okay. Great." She headed for the door. "I guess I'll take my shower now."

"Cassie."

She turned and looked at him.

"You were right last night," he said. "It's best if you sleep in your own bed. It's best, too, that you understand that I have no intention of making this marriage other than temporary."

She nodded seriously. Yet he had the irrational conviction that she wasn't really listening.

One week later Cassie was convinced that Gideon's secretary had missed her calling. She should have been a drill instructor. Or maybe, Cassie thought, as she stared out the window in Gideon's office, a forgotten pile of rolled maps in her arms, Mrs. Pittinger should have been a counter-intelligence agent. She was uncannily good at catching Cassie woolgathering. But wouldn't the secretary's skill have been better used in the service of her country, trolling for foreign agents instead of an occasionally absent-minded clerk-trainee?

She sighed. Nothing was going right, not here or at home.

Not that she and Gideon argued. Oh, no. She didn't see him enough to argue with him. Between business dinners and working late, Gideon managed to avoid being home much. When he did show up at the apartment he was polite, damn him, and went back to his bedroom after exchanging a few courtesies. She knew what he was doing, of course. He was trying to keep from taking her up on the offer her body kept making in spite of her. Try as she would, Cassie knew she wasn't able to keep her feelings to herself. No doubt all he had to do was look at her to know how she reacted to him.

Desperately. Wildly. Cassie had always wanted Gideon. Living with him, seeing him every morning and every night, just built that craving until she was dizzy with it. Cold showers, she'd discovered, were highly overrated.

Not that *he* would know. The current of desire might be a floodwater for her, hurtling her from rock to rock and threatening to pull her under, but as far as she could tell, Gideon had stayed safely on the bank, watching her flounder. If he was avoiding her, it was because he didn't want to take advantage, damn him.

As for the office—well, if Cassie had worried about Gideon giving her preferential treatment because she was his wife, she needn't have. He treated her exactly like he would have any newly hired clerk. He ignored her. So here she stood, alone in his office while he attended to some mysterious business, staring out the window at the city below.

Windows and distance. Gideon's courtesy was like window

glass. It let him see the world while staying remote, untouched. And yet she was convinced that deep inside he was badly in need of the very contact he'd closed himself off from. Shifting her load to one arm, Cassie pressed her palm against the cool glass, and thought about Vegas.

Gideon had thrilled Cassie by holding on to her pretty much from the minute she'd agreed to marry him, as if he hadn't wanted to risk losing her. On the plane they'd held hands. When they'd checked into the Treasure Island Resort, Gideon had kept her close to his side. In the dizzying newness of that contact, Cassie had forgotten to be afraid.

Once they'd gotten in the cab, though, to go to the courthouse for the marriage license, Ryan had ridden up front with the cab driver, leaving the back seat to Gideon and Cassie. And Gideon had stopped touching her.

Cassie had stared out the side window. The glass had reflected the black of the night back at her, brilliantly gemmed with the garish lights of the Strip. She was in Las Vegas, she'd told herself, on her way to the Marriage License Bureau, and in another hour or so, she would be married to Gideon Wilde.

She was crazy.

"Are you scared?" Gideon asked.

"No, of course not." She rubbed her stomach, where a tight ball of nerves lodged. It wasn't too late to change her mind. Then she looked at him.

"Why the hell not?" he demanded. He was close. Closer than she'd realized. The lights of the Strip slid across the liquid surface of his beautiful eyes, just as they had the car window. "You're supposed to be scared," he told her, his tone as definite as if his words weren't slurred around the edges. "What kind of a marriage is it if the bride isn't scared?"

"What about the groom?" she asked, rubbing the place where a knot of twisting worry-snakes wriggled uncomfortably.

"Brides should be scared," he insisted stubbornly.

Even drunk, she realized, Gideon couldn't admit to fear. But it was there. The rush of tenderness she felt soothed the snakes in her middle as she took his hand. "I am a little frightened," she said. "Gideon?"

"Hmm?" He looked out the window, as if barely aware of her beside him.

"Were you scared about marrying Melissa?"

For a long moment she didn't think he was going to answer. "No," he said at last. "I wasn't. Not the least bit nervous." His hand tightened around hers. "It's okay if you're scared, Cassie."

Now Cassie stared out another window without seeing it. She saw her hand pressed against the glass—the cadmium yellow cuticles, the streak of alizarin crimson on her thumb and the gold ring on the third finger.

Did he remember? she thought wistfully. He'd forgotten a lot of that night, but did he at least remember their taxi ride, and what he'd said to her?

She turned to study the wall across from Gideon's desk. The painting she'd started Sunday would go there when it was finished, right where that boring clock was. Where Gideon would look up and see it and think of her.

"When the big hand's on the twelve, you can go home," said a raspy female voice. "Until then, you're supposed to get some work done."

Cassie jolted, dropping three of the maps she'd forgotten she was holding. Mrs. Pittinger stood just inside the door, looking impatient from the toes of her small, elegant feet to the frizzed tips of her varicolored hair.

"How do you do that?" Cassie complained, bending to retrieve the maps. "I didn't even hear the door open."

"Huh. You wouldn't have heard a brass band just now. Mooning over Gideon, I suppose." She frowned. "It had better be Gideon you're mooning over."

"I was thinking about a painting," she said with dignity as she crossed to the map stand and started putting the maps up. "When I'm not at the office loading your barges and toting your bales, I paint. I certainly don't spend all of my time thinking about Gideon."

Mrs. Pittinger's lips may have twitched. Or maybe Cassie was just distracted by their color. They were a vivid orange today, which made an interesting statement against skin the color and texture of old leather. "Just try to use all your creativity in your painting from now on," she said, "instead of your filing."

"I found that letter again, didn't I?" Cassie slid the last map into place and smiled. She couldn't help it. Mrs. Pittinger looked so suspicious. "Don't worry," she said as she crossed the room. "I think I'm getting the hang of how things are done around here."

"Really. Then I suppose you had a good reason to put every one of those land maps in with the rolled seismic sections?"

Cassie glanced back at the map rack that wasn't a map rack after all, and sighed.

At eleven-thirty Cassie had the telephone propped between her ear and her shoulder while she hunt-and-peck typed a letter in the cubbyhole she laughingly called her office. The tiny room held a desk and chair, a phone, a computer, a wastebasket, and a huge abstract painting, her favorite from her cubist period, exploding with reds and yellows.

She'd decided she liked the computer. It had an almost infinite capacity for undoing her mistakes. "I'd better not join you and Mo for lunch today, Jaya. I need to finish typing this letter."

"We can make it a late lunch. How long is the letter?"

"I won't know that until I've finished typing it, now, will I? Just a sec." Cassie hit the Play button on the tape recorder, listened to exactly one sentence, and shut it off. "How do you spell sedimentary?"

"How would I know? Take a guess and let the spell checker sort it out."

"Okay." Cassie was pretty sure she could figure out how to use the spell checker. Eventually.

"So how's the job going?" Jaya asked. "You note, I hope,

that I'm restraining myself from asking how the marriage is going."

"The job's fine. Of course, my boss hates me, but—"

"Gideon hates you?"

"Not him, Mrs. Pittinger, and I don't know if she actually *hates* me, but she thinks I'm a lousy clerk—"

"You are."

"—and that I'm an opportunist or something, and tricked Gideon into marrying me. As for Gideon, he treats me like any other employee, which is not what I had in mind at all." *S-e-d-a-m-e-n-t-e-r-y,* she typed. It didn't look right. "I thought if we worked together I'd be around him more." She needed to be around him enough for him to fall in love with her...or for her to accept that it wasn't going to happen. Cassie had promised herself she would get out of the marriage if it became obvious he wasn't ever going to love her. "So far it isn't working," she finished glumly.

"You should make him jealous."

"I don't think that's a good plan, Jaya."

"Why not? I bet if you'd fan those flames a little you could get Gideon to stop ignoring you."

"Oh, no. Absolutely not." She deleted back to the *a* and tried an *e. S-e-d-e-m-e-n-t-e-r-y?* "I told you—oh!" Cassie straightened as she caught sight of movement in the doorway. "Mrs. Pittinger."

"Gideon called," the other woman said, bristling with disapproval. "I would have put him through to you, but your line has been busy for some time. I took a message."

Cassie hastily told Jaya they'd get together for lunch another day, and hung up. "Yes?" she asked as she faced her boss, lifting her eyebrows in an effort to imitate Gideon's chilly courtesy.

"Your face will freeze that way if you're not careful," the woman said.

It was so much what Cassie's grandmother might have said that she burst out laughing.

Mrs. Pittinger nodded as if Cassie had just confirmed something. "Gideon wants you to meet him for lunch at Grishom's," she said, naming an exclusive downtown restaurant. "Miss Wilde will be joining you."

Cassie's brows pulled together in puzzlement. "Miss Wilde?"

"His aunt, Eleanor Wilde," Mrs. Pittinger said, adding with what seemed like grim pleasure, "Watch out for the old witch. I don't think she's going to like you."

Six

Grishom's customers didn't have to worry about finding nouvelle cuisine on the menu. The eighty-year-old restaurant featured beef and plenty of it, served rare enough to dodge out of the way if you weren't fast with your fork. The chandeliers were as old as the restaurant, and beautiful. The carpet looked about the same age, and much uglier.

"I'll have a T-bone, medium rare, but don't put it on until—" Gideon hesitated briefly "—until my wife arrives." He folded the menu and handed it to the hovering waiter.

"Your *wife*," the woman across from him said as soon as the waiter was gone. "Tell me, Gideon, was this some sort of delayed adolescent rebellion?"

Age suited Eleanor Wilde. White hair and soft, crepey skin went well with the delicacy of her facial bones, her long, narrow hands and fragile wrists. She kept her hair short, in the same practical style she'd worn ever since Gideon could remember. She'd never admitted to being aware that the style was also flattering, that anything fussier would have overwhelmed her fragile features, but Gideon suspected she knew. Or maybe he just wanted to believe that somewhere inside her lingered a failing as human as vanity. "I've known Cassie for years," he said in oblique answer to her question.

"You've known my friend Barbara for years, too, but you didn't run off to Las Vegas and marry her. *Vegas.*" She shuddered.

Gideon had known his aunt would be appalled by his marriage. He'd put off calling her, excused by the fact that she'd been out of town until yesterday. "You've already made your opinion of my actions clear," he said levelly, "and when you insisted on meeting Cassie right away, I agreed. But I will not allow you to abuse her because you are disappointed in me."

"I'm perfectly capable of civilized behavior." Her expression indicated that she had doubts about him, however. "Oh, Gideon. If you'd just waited, I'm sure you and Melissa could have patched things up."

"Doesn't it cross your mind that I might not have wanted to patch things up with a woman who jilted me less than a week before the wedding?" Instead he'd run off with Cassie…who was driving him slowly crazy.

Eventually, he assured himself, his craving for her would dim. Then they could be friends again. He had to find a way to make that happen. Only now, with that friendship endangered by marriage and lust, did he understand how important it had been to him to know that even if he didn't see Cassie often, she was out there, that he could pick up a phone and talk to her if he needed.

He'd never done it, of course. But he'd liked knowing that he could.

"Breaking the engagement was an unfortunate decision on Melissa's part," Eleanor conceded. "But this—this marriage of yours is more than unfortunate."

His eyes narrowed. "Be careful. Be very careful."

"Oh, I'm not going to insult your bride when I haven't yet met her. But the family, Gideon. Her mother is a waitress, for

God's sake. Hardly a mark of intellectual prowess, is it? And the brother, whom I have met several times—''

"Is my friend.''

She nodded impatiently. "I know, and I've nothing against him personally. He's even rather successful, I understand. But he's also emotional. Impetuous. And Cassandra, you tell me, is some sort of artist. Between that, my knowledge of her brother and the fact that she was willing to run off with you at a moment's notice, do you wonder that I have made certain assumptions about her? A touch of madness might be necessary in an artist, but, Gideon, is this the sort of bloodline you want to mix with your own?''

He knew what she meant. He knew, and that knowledge chilled him from the bones out, a cold that came from so deep inside he supposed it was part of his soul as well as his flesh.

The part he'd inherited from his father.

Fortunately he didn't have to answer. He saw Cassie following the maître d' across the dining room. She wore one of her ''office'' outfits. The distinction, he'd learned, had more to do with which of her clothes had oil paint on them than with style. Today's selection was orange. Not a moderate russet or subdued bronze, but true, flaming orange in a dress that somehow crossed a Roman toga with baby doll pajamas. It was short and sexy and as understated as a shout.

If Cassie had stayed up all night picking exactly the wrong thing to wear to meet Eleanor Wilde, she couldn't have done a better job. If her goal had been to get Gideon's heart rate up and his blood heating, she'd managed that, too.

Gideon didn't notice the corner of his mouth turning up as Cassie approached them, but his aunt did.

A touch of despair wrapped clammy hands around Eleanor Wilde's throat. If he actually cherishes some sort of passion for that creature, she thought, what will I do? She thrust the doubt away.

She would do whatever had to be done, as she always had. She studied the young woman Gideon had so impulsively married while he stood and introduced them. *Transparent*, she thought, correctly interpreting the nerves that had Cassie's hands opening and closing on the purse she clutched. Probably guileless as well, she decided, looking at the friendly expression. A pity. That ended her hope that the girl might be an opportunist who could be bought off.

The lunch confirmed all of Eleanor's fears. Cassandra O'Grady—Eleanor could not bring herself to add "Wilde"—possessed all the charm of any young animal. She was lovely, impulsive, by turns awkward and intuitive, and as naturally, compellingly physical as the *houris* a devout Muslim dreamed of finding waiting for him in Paradise.

Eleanor was aware that her nephew considered her an unemotional woman, her only passion, dry as it might be, given to the orderly god of mathematics, which she taught at a local college. He was wrong. If math was the organizing principle of her cosmos, Gideon was the sun her solar system revolved around. She had never allowed him to suspect this, of course. Such an indulgence could easily have ruined him when he was younger, and besides, the habit of reticence was too deeply ingrained.

But she would do anything for him. Anything. And this disastrous marriage of his, she concluded, long before she rose to take polite leave of her nephew and his charming young wife, was going to tax her abilities to their limit.

"I thought the lunch went well, didn't you, Gideon?" Cassie asked anxiously as they made their way down a crowded sidewalk to the parking garage that held their cars. Gideon would go back to the office while Cassie went home to paint.

Home? Well, Cassie thought, Gideon's apartment wasn't quite that yet, but she was working on it. "Your aunt may still have some reservations about us, but that's only natural under the circumstances. And her friend is going to give us a party. That indicates Eleanor has basically accepted the marriage, don't you think?" Cassie paused when she saw the man in ragged clothes on the corner. The placard around his neck read Homeless: Will Work for Food. "Gideon..."

"I'm not going to give him a job, Cassie," Gideon said mildly. He grabbed her elbow as if he knew she'd been about to dart forward. "No," he told her.

"But, Gideon—"

"I'll give him something."

He did, and they argued the rest of the way to the parking garage over whether the man had really wanted work and felt demeaned by Gideon's handout, or whether he was a cagey beggar who knew perfectly well no one in downtown Dallas was going to offer him work, but a few tender souls might give him money. In the process, Cassie forgot her question and the fact that Gideon hadn't answered it.

She almost forgot the uneasy feeling she'd had on first meeting Eleanor Wilde.

The painting didn't go well that afternoon. After fighting with it for an hour, Cassie gave up and pulled out stretcher bars, canvas and gesso and occupied herself with the mindless work of building and preparing canvasses. She succeeded in losing herself in the repetitious chore so thoroughly that for the first time she forgot to put anything on for supper. Of course Gideon chose that day to actually come home on time.

That night, on the one-week anniversary of their marriage, they ate take-out hamburgers in front of the TV. Gideon flipped a coin to determine whether they would watch a sitcom Cassie liked or the nature special he preferred. Cassie won...sort of. They watched her show. They even laughed together, though they sat apart. Cassie felt warm and comfortable in spite of the hum of desire just beneath her skin.

As soon as the show was over, though, Gideon vanished to his bedroom with his briefcase for the rest of the evening.

Cassie was in her cubbyhole at 8:10 the next morning, struggling with the letter she hadn't finished the day before, when Mrs. Pittinger steamed in. "Well?" the woman demanded. "Did you get along with Miss Wilde?"

"It's Dr. Wilde," Cassie said peevishly, "which I'm sure you're aware of, and might have mentioned yesterday before

I left.'' Cassie had addressed the woman incorrectly, making it clear how little Gideon had told her about his family. Or himself.

"I'll bet she said she reserves the title for her students, didn't she? Well, don't you believe it. She likes to have that 'doctor' hung out at the front of her name.'' Mrs. Pittinger gave a satisfied nod, then amazed Cassie by looking around and adding, "You need another chair in here for people to sit in.''

Cassie's eyebrows went up. "But that would encourage people to actually speak to me. Distract me from my duties.''

"Ha. As if you needed any excuse to get distracted. So, is that the type of painting you do?'' She moved over to study the huge canvas that took up much of the wall behind Cassie.

"My work's more representational these days.''

"Hmm. I suppose I should see something recent, then, but I like this. Spontaneous, yet with hints of form emerging from the chaos. Nice brushwork.''

Cassie stared, amazed all over again. Slowly she smiled. "You like modern art?''

"My second husband was Adolfo Madieros.''

"Madieros…oh, the sculptor! He did those huge mixed-media pieces back in the eighties, didn't he? Though I hear he's gone back to clay now. I met him once at a party. He—'' She broke off, remembering the egotistical little man's crude invitation. "He's a very talented artist,'' she finished diplomatically.

Mrs. Pittinger snorted. "Tried to pick you up, did he?''

Cassie grinned and relaxed. For whatever reason, Mrs. Pittinger had apparently decided to accept her. "I thought he was an obnoxious little beast, and told him so. It didn't seem to faze him.''

She nodded. "That's Adolfo. Splendid sculptor. Those hands…still, he was quite the worst husband I ever had. Now, Gideon,'' she said, "will make you a very good husband, once you get him to loosen up and fall in love with you.''

Cassie noticed her mouth was hanging open, so she used it

to say, "I suppose you're going to tell me how I should go about that."

"No. If you can't take care of it yourself, you're not the woman he needs, after all. Although I am beginning to have some hope." She moved to the doorway on her dainty feet. "At least you kept him from marrying that Barbie doll he was engaged to. His aunt selected her for him, you know."

"She did?" Cassie was dubious. She couldn't imagine Gideon calmly agreeing to follow his aunt's dictates, or being manipulated into it, either.

"Don't underestimate her. A brilliant woman, Eleanor Wilde. But devious. You have that letter finished yet? The one I gave you yesterday?"

"Uh...I was working on it when you came in."

Mrs. Pittinger glanced at the monitor and sighed. "I had so hoped to get one who typed this time," she said sadly as she left.

When the phone rang late that afternoon, Cassie's hands were slimy with chicken innards. She rinsed them hurriedly and grabbed the receiver. "Hello?"

"I hope you haven't already started cooking," Gideon told her, "because I'll be late tonight."

She looked at the bowl of stuffing and the disemboweled roasting hen that sat on the counter. Her lips tightened. "Now why would I have started cooking anything? It's only twenty after five," she said. They'd been married one week and one day, she thought, and he'd been home for dinner exactly twice. "Let me guess. You're still at the office, and something has come up."

"Yes." There was a long pause. "I expect I'll be home between eight and nine. Don't hold dinner for me. I'll have a sandwich or something up here."

"Good idea," she said approvingly. "Because I doubt I'll be here when you get home. Maybe I'll go bar-hopping," she said, jerking at the ties on the apron she wore, "or maybe I'll go see Jaya perform at the club. Who knows?" Angrily she pulled the apron off and tossed it on the floor. "I might meet someone and have a wild, adulterous affair."

Dead silence. Finally he said coolly, "I expect I'll see you tonight, then. If you decide to come home."

The click in her ear told her he'd hung up. Furious, she stamped out of the kitchen. The chicken could just rot, she decided. It could sit there on the counter and stink and make him feel bad for...for what? she asked herself as she paced back and forth in front of the window. For not changing his life around to suit her, the way she'd been bending herself double trying to please him?

No wonder she'd had trouble painting lately, she thought, disgusted, and flopped down on one of the couches. Again this afternoon she'd put her paints away early—and why? Because she'd been planning dinner. Worrying about whether Gideon liked squash, and wondering if she had tarragon. *It took me long enough to notice that I'm being an idiot,* she thought, scowling at the ceiling.

No more. She sat up. She'd still cook sometimes, sure. She liked cooking. But she wasn't going to knock herself out planning and preparing meals every night, when he had little intention of being home to eat them.

Tonight she'd go out, just like she'd said. She hurried to the kitchen and put away the chicken and the bowl of dressing, because she couldn't stand to waste food. In the bathroom she pulled off her paint-spattered T-shirt and dropped it and her ratty shorts on the floor, to make up for having tidied the kitchen.

Maybe she wasn't going to do *exactly* what she'd said, she admitted as she zipped up a clean pair of jeans, then fastened silver earrings shaped like pinwheels to her ears. She leaned more toward shopping than adulterous affairs.

As she closed the front door behind her, she mused *It isn't easy, to court a man who is determined to avoid you.* But Cassie was stubborn. She didn't expect life to be easy.

* * *

At 9:55 that night Cassie let herself in the front door. Her evening hadn't been completely useless, since she carried three bags with store logos that held one ridiculously expensive art book, three pairs of earrings, a purple sweatshirt for her and a pale yellow shirt for Gideon. Unfortunately she still didn't have a plan for how to get Gideon's attention long enough to make him fall in love with her.

The living room was dark. The kitchen was dark. But something soft with lots of strings was playing on the stereo, and light leaked from under the closed door to Gideon's bedroom. Cassie stood in the short entry hall, watching that ribbon of light and trying to decide if she wanted to fight, forgive, or just take a bath.

His door opened. The light streaming from behind turned him mysterious—large, dark and dangerous. "Apparently you decided to come home after all," he said evenly.

The wiggly feeling the sight of him set off in her stomach did not please her. She frowned as she stepped down into the living room and tossed the shopping bags on one of the couches. "I told you I'd be out."

"Yes." With his face shadowed, his expression was completely unreadable. "You did, didn't you?" He turned and went back into his room.

Temper sparked. Trying to suppress it, she headed for his door. "You're not going to ask where I've been, are you? Or yell at me, or call me names, even though you're obviously angry. I tell you, Gideon, you need some major training in how to have a fight." As she crossed the doorway into his room, she decided she was just the person to teach him.

Three steps into his room she jerked to a stop. Fear, total and unreasoning, slammed into her.

He was packing. A garment bag lay flat on the bed, its long zipper open so that she could see at least one of his suits was already tucked inside. Even as her breath caught in her chest, he bent and slid a shirt onto one of the bag's hangers.

He was *leaving.*

Dizzy, she automatically gulped down a breath. Her hand,

pressed flat to her chest, picked up the panicky thudding of her heart. "What are you doing?"

"I think that's obvious." He didn't pause, didn't look at her, as he tucked socks into the pocket at the bottom of the bag.

"It's obvious that you're packing. What I don't know is *why*."

"Try thinking for once," he snapped, heading for the bathroom, "and see if the answer comes to you. If not, the practice won't hurt."

The temper that roared in now energized her. She dashed into the bathroom after him. "What kind of answer is that? I want to know, dammit—"

"What you *want*," he snapped, rounding on her so fast she jerked back, "means less than nothing at this moment. Do you know how I felt?" He grabbed her shoulders. "Do you have any idea how I felt when I came home and you weren't here?"

She stared up at him, slack-jawed. What was this? *Who* was this? Had she ever seen this crazy man scowling down at her whose fingers dug into her shoulders hard enough to hurt? He stood so close she saw herself reflected in the darkness of his eyes. So close she saw the shadow of his beard, felt the warmth of his breath as she stared up at his face, his expression transformed by the heat of his fury into something fierce and free. He looked primitive—as primitive as the hunger that coursed through her, pulsing heavy and low like the beat of native drums.

She swayed toward him.

He was going to kiss her. For one suspended moment she was certain of it. She watched him struggle for control, saw the battle in his face, felt it in the hands that tightened brutally on her shoulders...then let go. He inhaled slowly. Eyes that had blazed with fury chilled, taking on the ungiving sheen of black ice at night. He pulled away.

Then he turned his back on her.

If she could have moved, she would have dragged him back to her. If she could have spoken she would have demanded that he never, ever turn away from her like that again. But her breath shuddered through her too unsteadily for speech, and her knees were wrecked.

He opened the medicine cabinet.

"Gideon?" she managed.

"There's an emergency at the Port-au-Prince well," he said, referring to a lease owned by an investor group he'd put together. He didn't look at her as he checked his shaving kit. "They hit a high-pressure gas pocket. There was a blowout, and one of the roustabouts was injured."

"Oh, God. Is he okay?"

"He's in the hospital with a minor concussion. But I have to go."

She nodded, her brain clearing slowly. Yes, Gideon would have to go. He would want to see the injured man personally, if he could. Then he'd want to find out what went wrong and who was at fault—that, very definitely. "Why didn't you tell me?" she asked softly. "You know what I thought, why I was angry. Why didn't you tell me you had a real emergency when you called?"

He met her gaze, his eyes flat, unrevealing. "I didn't hear about the accident until an hour ago. I didn't know about it when I called."

"I see." She tried to swallow her hurt. It went down like ground glass, spreading the pain. "So until then, you were just avoiding me. The way you have been ever since you made the mistake of marrying me." Since she couldn't possibly let herself cry, not with him watching her so steadily, she held her head high.

"Don't." The ice covering his expression cracked, and she realized that the heat, the fury, weren't gone at all. "Don't look like that, dammit."

His control broke so suddenly. In two steps he had his hands on her again. Her heart jolted, and maybe it was from fear this time. This time, he didn't think, didn't struggle. He took her mouth with the certainty and hunger of a beast starved for days and then teased with the promise of a meal. His hands raced over her, hot hands, hard and hasty with his own need.

Her body surrendered instantly. Her mind dove off into space—black, endless, terrifying. Had she thought she knew desire? This was different. Darker, like the taste of his mouth, like the ache his hunger called from the center of her being. He kneaded her breast and she shuddered with the force of what he unleashed. Yet she'd been with him. God, she'd lain in his arms after making love, and if that had been a hasty joining, with him too drunk, too little aware of what he did or with whom, what of it? She still knew the feel of him, didn't she? And he'd kissed her. The night he left, that first night in his apartment, he'd kissed her and made her weak with wanting him.

Yet this was nothing she'd ever felt before.

When he slid his leg between hers, she moaned and pressed against it, needing to be closer to him and what only he could give her.

When he pulled his head back, she waited for him to kiss her elsewhere, to take her clothes off or carry her to bed or just sink with her to the floor and put himself inside her. His chest shuddered against hers with the force of his breaths, yet he did nothing. Nothing at all. Slowly, disbelievingly, she opened her eyes.

He held her up. With his thigh between hers and his hand on her bottom he kept her from falling while his eyes burned down at her. "Don't follow me around," he said, his voice low and raw. "Don't smile at me and coax me to spend time with you. Don't fix my favorite meals and do all those other little wifely things, pretending to take care of me."

He slid his leg out from between hers. She felt horribly uncertain of her ability to continue standing. The ground beneath her feet had never seemed so treacherous before.

He drew his hand slowly up from her bottom to her waist in a long, controlled caress that aroused her as thoroughly as it made her want to cry—maybe because he *was* controlled again, while she just kept unraveling.

"Don't hover, don't smile, don't pretend," he told her grimly. "Unless you're prepared to *be* a wife, a real wife, and to take care of me in the way I need." He grabbed her hand and pressed it firmly, deliberately, to his groin. When she jerked, reflexively trying to free her hand, he only pressed her fingers tighter around him. He was large and hard and throbbing. "Grow up, little girl. We aren't playing house. You won't get candlelight and lies from me, and I don't want them from you. You know what I do want, though, don't you?" He rubbed his pelvis against her captive hand, and she hated the rush of heat that made her dizzy, limp, his. "Are you ready to oblige me, Cassie?"

He might as well have asked if she was ready to service him. Heat and hunger mixed with the wave of humiliation that crested over her head, drowning her in a briny backwash of feeling. She cried out incoherently, pulling on her hand.

"If not," he said softly, "you'd better get out of here. Now."

The second he released her hand she fled.

Seven

Gideon stayed away for two days and two nights. He talked to the tool pusher at the well and to the injured roughneck, and during the daylight hours he took care of what had to be done. At night he went to his hotel room and didn't drink.

For the first time in his life, he had some idea of how seductively alcohol must have called to his father. But because it would have been too easy, he couldn't seek comfort there.

He didn't, after all, deserve comfort.

On the third night he lay in the center of the king-size hotel bed while some stupid television show filled the air with voices and canned laughter. Gideon didn't watch much TV. He certainly never turned the "idiot box" on just to fill up the silence of his solitude.

Yet tonight he was so much more alone than usual, maybe because he could hardly stand to be in the same room as himself.

What had he done?

The noise from the TV wasn't enough to drown out the

remembered sound of Cassie's moan, breathy and helpless with desire, when he'd pressed his thigh up into her center. The flickering light from the TV didn't do a damned thing to shut out the sight of her face, desperately vulnerable, while he used words like blows to strip her of any illusions she might have held about him and what he had to offer her.

There must have been a thousand other ways, better, kinder ways, to persuade her that he could give her his hunger, his fidelity and a comfortable life financially, and that was all. There wasn't anything else in him, dammit, and that's one reason he'd been so angry with the way she kept smiling at him, cooking for him…hoping. Damn her, she'd been hoping, and he knew it. But he hadn't looked for other ways to convince her of the truth. He'd wanted only to make her leave as fast as possible, before he grabbed her and had sex with her there on the floor, losing himself in the headiest rush any addict ever killed for.

God, how he'd wanted her.

So he'd lied. Not overtly, maybe, but tacitly. The same way he'd been lying to himself. Because if all he'd felt for her was a physical need, he could have handled it—would have handled it, quite thoroughly, by taking her straight to bed, where he could do them both some good.

But his needs hadn't been only physical. That's what had scared him. That's why he'd attacked with words, with a crudeness that, at last, had made her beautiful eyes fill with tears just before she ran from him as if he'd sprouted horns and a tail.

Gideon thought about how he'd felt something like this once before. Felt it, suppressed it, believed that he'd beaten it. He lay on his back on the quilted spread of that big, empty bed in a very nice hotel room in a small Louisiana town and thought about a young girl's first high school prom.…

The sky was blue, that particular, piercing blue it sometimes wears in early spring, a color almost too pure to believe after the gray of winter. Gideon lay on his back in the prickly grass of a bank that sloped down to a dry creekbed. The earth beneath him still held on to the chill of winter, but the cold was as refreshing as the brilliant color overhead. He was at least fifty feet from the edge of the trailer park where his friend's family lived, and alone. That was what he wanted at the moment. Over the past three and a half years he'd come here with Ryan often enough that it was almost like having a family himself—close enough that he didn't worry about offending anyone if he wanted to lie in the grass and grab a little solitude.

One more semester—a matter of weeks now—and he was through. Out. Graduated from college, and with honors. The honors mattered to his aunt, and he felt he owed them to her. He didn't think he owed her another two to four years, though, pursuing the advanced degree she wanted him to have.

Gideon wanted wealth a great deal more than he wanted academic recognition. He had a pretty clear idea of what money could buy and what it couldn't. He thought he could get by just fine with those things that were available for cold, hard cash, because those were the things he could depend on.

He would have to make his own way, of course. His aunt had money, but he never considered asking her to risk some of it on his plans. Aunt Eleanor had seemed truly rich to him ten years ago, when he'd first gone to live with her, but he knew now her wealth was limited. She had her professor's salary, of course, and she had her share of the inheritance, sensibly invested, the same amount that his father had drunk and gambled away long ago. Gideon understood that the safe, the practical, would always be Eleanor Wilde's way. He knew that way had value. But you didn't go from dead broke, as he'd been, to rich by playing it safe, which was why Gideon had chosen geophysics for his major.

The oil business was one huge gamble, and a lot more tax write-offs were drilled than gushers. But Gideon figured that if he gambled cold—not hot and impulsive like his father—if he kept his head and knew going in what he was risking, he could make it.

He heard footsteps in the dry grass, slow, dragging footsteps that scuffed along unhappily. He knew who it was before he heard her voice.

At first all he could make out among her mutterings was something about a dress and "every other girl" and "the dance." But as she got nearer he heard her more clearly.

"I *could* have had the money for it, too, but no-o-o. 'Worry about your schoolwork,'" Cassie whined in the falsetto that teens use to imitate motherly injunctions, as if motherhood reset the vocal chords to a higher, more irritating register. "'You are not getting a part-time job while those algebra grades are so low.' As if *that*," she declared passionately to what she assumed was empty space as she stopped at the top of the bank, "would make me care more about stupid algebra!"

Gideon heard her foot kick out at the grass, so maybe it shouldn't have surprised him when dirt rained down in his face. "Hey!" He sat up, brushing the dirt off.

"What are you doing here?" she demanded. She stood there, hands on her skinny, jeans-covered hips, and glared down at him. Her bright hair was gathered haphazardly into a ponytail, and her chameleon eyes were nearly the same green as her shirt. Temper, he knew, had that effect on them.

Gideon smiled. The youngest member of the small O'Grady clan always charmed him, even when she was doing her best to be rude and nasty. "Eavesdropping," he said. "I snuck out here and lay down where you wouldn't see me just so I could listen in on your monologue."

"Well," she said, and her frown twitched at one corner, as if she was working hard to keep it in place, "that was tricky of you." She went down the bank and dropped onto the ground beside him, crossing her arms over her raised knees. "It's just not fair, that's all."

He stretched out again, propped up on his elbow this time. "Very little is."

"Yes, but—oh, I know you don't care about dresses and stuff. You're a guy. But I'd have plenty of money for a dress,

something really nice, if Mom would just listen.'' Her hand
absently plucked at the grass, grabbing and discarding tufts.
"Ryan has worked since he was in high school, and she thinks
that's great. I told her," Cassie said with a serious nod, "that
she was being sexist."

He managed to contain his amusement. "Did you, now.
And what did she say?"

"That gender had nothing to do with it. Just algebra." She
tossed a handful of dead grass into the air and leaned back on
her elbows. "Algebra stinks." She heaved a huge sigh.

The way she was leaning back, the motion of her sigh lifted
her chest dramatically. His eyes involuntarily went to her
breasts, draped with soft, clingy cotton. *Cassie has breasts?*
Very pretty breasts, too, small but shapely, and she must not
be wearing a bra because he could see the little bumps her
nipples made—

He tore his eyes away, appalled. How could he be thinking
about Cassie's nipples? She wasn't even supposed to have
breasts. What business did she have getting breasts, real
breasts, the kind that made his breath feel hot and trapped in
his chest while his jeans got tight?

He pulled up one leg, shielding his reaction from her as best
he could. But even now, with his eyes fixed once more on that
ridiculously blue sky, he kept reacting. "So you're still having
problems with algebra?"

"I've got a C," she said. "It's not a very high C, but I'm
passing. So you'd think she could trust me to know what I'm
doing, wouldn't you? I really need a job, Gideon."

She sounded so forlorn that he made a mistake. He looked
at her again.

She was flat on her back in the grass now, not watching
him. Freckles were sprinkled like fairy dust over skin as soft
as butter and more pure than the sky overhead. Her lashes
were red-gold in the sunlight, and her bottom lip drooped.

He wanted to take that lip between his teeth. To slip his
tongue between her lips.

Horrified, he looked away again. He was, he told himself,

years older and decades more experienced than the sprite lying so innocently next to him. He could control himself. He could make sure she never knew. "You muttered something about a dance." His voice came out too low. Husky. He prayed she wouldn't notice or understand.

Maybe his prayers were answered, because she sat up and destroyed more grass while she chattered about the dance. This wasn't just a regular dance, it seemed. No one wore dresses to a regular dance. No, little Cassie was worried about having a nice dress for the prom. She already had a date.

"Wait a minute." He sat up, frowning. "You can't be old enough for the prom yet. Or for dating."

"Honestly, you sound just like Ryan. I'm *sixteen*, Gideon. I've got my license and everything. I'm plenty old enough to date."

Old enough to—*no,* he told the most willful, impudent part of his body, which had leapt to full attention. She is *not* old enough. Cassie was just a kid still, and he was not going to let the sweet tide of lust singing through his veins make him see her any differently.

What was wrong with him? How could he be feeling this way?

He sat up suddenly, keeping his legs cocked to hide his lap. "I've got some extra money," he said. "If you're worried about getting a nice dress, I could help." When she didn't say anything, he knew he'd given himself away somehow. He wanted to crawl off and die. "Cassie..."

"I suppose," she said in a crisp, formal little voice, "you're being nice, and I should thank you. But I would have thought, Gideon, that we were better friends than that."

She thought they were better friends than that—and that he was being *nice?*

"How could you? How could you think I was fishing for some kind of—of—*charity?*" She pushed to her feet. "Maybe my mother can't buy me exactly the dress I want, and maybe I shouldn't have been whining about it, but that doesn't mean I want a handout!"

"Uh..." he said cleverly, and looked at her.

She was swatting at the sleeves of her shirt, knocking off bits of dried grass, and frowning like a spinster schoolteacher. "It's not like you're just rolling in money yourself," she said. "And even if you were, that wouldn't make it right."

"No," he agreed, flooded with a relief so profound he felt giddy. She didn't know. "I guess I just wasn't thinking."

"Well. That's something, to hear you almost admit you were wrong." She grinned suddenly. "I guess I forgive you. Are you coming?" She turned and started back up the bank. "Mom's not cooking tonight, Ryan is. So it's safe to show up for supper." At the top of the bank she paused and dusted the back of her jeans, swishing her bottom slightly as she did.

Her round, curvy little bottom. Gideon managed not to groan as he fell back onto the ground again. "No," he said in as level a voice as he could find. "I think I'll stay out a little longer."

The sound track on the sitcom Gideon wasn't watching poured canned laughter into his pleasant, empty hotel room in a small town in Louisiana, and he grimaced. Funny how that one day stayed with him so clearly, even though there had been plenty of other times when his control had been more sorely tested. It had taken him better than two years to finally subjugate his body, and react normally—almost—to Cassie again. But what he remembered was that early spring day when he first saw Cassie as a woman.

Cassie *was* a woman now. And his wife. And willing, even eager, to be in his bed, whatever she said to the contrary, whatever room she was actually sleeping in. And Cassie, at age twenty-eight, was no more likely to marry a man for money than she had been willing at age sixteen to let Gideon buy her a prom dress.

He'd been wrong. One hundred percent wrong, and for the worst of reasons. He'd persuaded himself that Cassie owed him something because he was cross-eyed with lust and needed an excuse to act on it.

Gideon stared up at the ceiling and thought about a pure, improbably blue sky and a pure, improbably honest girl...and woman. Regardless of what Cassie had seemed to agree to, she hadn't married him for the financial support he could give her while she concentrated on her painting. When Gideon— not long from another woman's bed, and humiliated over being jilted—had asked her to marry him, she'd hoped for a great deal more than money from him.

But money was about all he could give her—money and the sexual hunger that kept him awake nights. Not the love she hoped for and deserved. Not the children she might want.

That would have to be enough, Gideon decided grimly. Somehow he would have to make it be enough, because he was pretty sure Cassie thought she was in love with him. Never mind that she was deluding herself. Never mind that he was being both a fool and a selfish bastard. He'd wanted her too long. This time, he wasn't stepping back. This time he would have her.

Gideon's plane landed at DFW at 9:14 the next morning. He went straight to his office, but for once his mind wasn't on business as he rode up in the elevator. He thought about Cassie, and if the ache of anxiety he felt wasn't quite like anything he'd felt before, he was certain he could contain it. Gideon was used to working against the odds, finding his way around or through obstacles. He just had to come up with a plan, a way to make up to Cassie for the way he'd behaved. He had to figure out what she needed. Once he knew what she needed, he would get it for her.

At 10:20 he stopped at his secretary's desk. Mrs. Pittinger looked worse than usual. Her hair stood straight up in agitated little spikes, and her mouth was a bright, carmine red today. She glared at him. "It's about time you got here."

He raised one eyebrow, a trick he knew irritated her. "I told you what time my plane would arrive this morning. Were you expecting me to teleport here directly?"

"You should have been here ten minutes ago."

"Traffic was heavy," he said, puzzled by her attitude. If something had been wrong, she would have already told him. "Ask Cassie to step into my office, would you?" he said, and started to turn away.

"She isn't here."

A sensation like vertigo struck him. He didn't recognize it as fear. Because it was strong, too strong, he fought it back. "What? Where—is she sick?"

"Not that I know of. And," she said belligerently, "if you have to ask me where your sweet young wife is and whether she's sick or not, I'd say you haven't been much of a husband so far."

Mrs. Pittinger was defending Cassie? Calling her sweet? Since when, in the long history of downtrodden clerks he'd hired for the dragon he called a secretary, had she ever taken their side about anything?

And where was Cassie? I'm not going to worry about her, he told himself. Just because he didn't know where Cassie was at the moment didn't mean that anything was wrong. Cassie was impulsive, but she wouldn't leave him just because they'd argued. Not without a word.

He ran a hand through his hair, unknowingly transforming it into a subdued version of Mrs. Pittinger's spikes. "I'll be in my office," he muttered. "If she calls...put her through right away if she calls." She was probably at the apartment, he told himself. If not, well, he could call Ryan to see if he knew where his sister was. He grimaced.

The changed expression on Mrs. Pittinger's face alerted him that someone had entered the reception area. He turned.

It was Cassie. Cassie, in tight, faded jeans, a denim jacket and a T-shirt that read Out of Body—Back in Fifteen Minutes. The crazy-quilt bag slung over her shoulder was sized halfway between a duffel bag and a purse.

She was smiling, dammit.

The first, swift kick of relief left him winded. Then furious.

She sauntered up to him, humming something under her breath. It sounded like "The Battle Hymn of the Republic."

He inhaled slowly. She smelled like flowers and rain. *Control,* he told himself. "Where in the hell have you been?"

The little fool tilted her head and smiled up at him as if she didn't notice how angry he was. Or didn't care. "Did you miss me?"

"You're supposed to be at work at eight o'clock. It's after ten. You didn't let anyone know where you were." He kept his voice even, spaced the words carefully.

"I was frying the chicken."

"Frying the—what are you doing?"

She'd eased up even closer to him and slid her small, warm hand up his chest. Her eyes laughed at him while she walked her fingers up his tie. "Hey, sailor," she said in a low, throaty voice, slanting him an outrageously sultry look and giving his tie a tug. "Wanna come with me for a good time?"

He was not going to laugh. Absolutely not. "You want to tell me what you're up to?"

"A major felony." Her other hand joined the first one on his tie. The movement of her knuckles against his chest sent smoky little bursts of heat prickling his skin even through the heavy cotton of his shirt. The sensation distracted him enough that it took him a moment to question just what she was doing with his tie. He looked down.

The little imp had the knot undone. She was taking his tie off, right there in the reception area. She was...stripping him?

Just the idea made the heat of desire explode into something darker and more fierce. Hunger roughened his voice. "You'd better tell me what you've got on your mind," he said, covering both her hands with one of his, holding them tight against his chest, "before I show you what's on mine."

The confusion he saw in her eyes when she raised them to his face pleased him. "I'm kidnapping you." She sounded slightly out of breath.

He stroked a finger along the inside of her wrist, where the hard gallop of her pulse told him what he needed to know. He didn't smile when he released her hands, but he was satisfied. Yes, he'd affected her.

For a second she didn't move, her eyes locked on his. Then she whipped his tie off and, as she stepped back, found another cheeky smile. "You're coming with me, mister. Don't struggle, or I might have to hurt you."

He wasn't going anywhere, of course. There was no way he was going to let her drag him off who knew where, to do who knew what...especially since he was pretty sure the "what" wasn't the activity his body was insisting on.

Fifteen minutes later, Gideon sat in the passenger seat of Cassie's ten-year-old Ford, pushing his foot to the floor where he wished he had a brake pedal. The back seat held a blanket and an old-fashioned picnic hamper that slid into the door when she turned sharply.

Cassie, he quickly learned, drove much like she lived. "Intuition has its place," he said, hanging on while she whipped across two congested lanes of traffic. "But it's not the best system for driving in heavy traffic."

She flashed him a quick grin and made an even quicker turn. "Not used to having someone else in the driver's seat, are you, Gideon? But it wouldn't be much of a kidnapping if I let you drive."

He wanted to tell her it wasn't any sort of a kidnapping, anyway, that he'd made a reasonable decision to go along with her. Except he couldn't remember quite how he'd come to make that decision. Still, he reminded himself, he had already decided to give Cassie whatever she needed. If she needed his company while she played Grand Prix driver through downtown Dallas... "I should have brought the cellular," he muttered. "Dammit, I can't believe I let you talk me out of bringing the cell phone."

"Relax." She reached over and patted his thigh, which affected his pulse rate even more than her driving did. "Emma will stay on top of things. She told you to submit decently to your abduction, didn't she?"

Emma? Who——? Good grief. Gideon had pretty much forgotten that his secretary even had a first name. He didn't think he'd ever heard anyone actually use it. "If you're referring to my traitorous secretary, you should bear in mind that I run the office, not her."

"Of course you do," Cassie said soothingly.

His lips threatened to twitch. He tightened them. "Mrs. Pittinger knew what you were up to, didn't she?" That was why she'd been irritated when he'd arrived late from the airport. She hadn't wanted him to miss Cassie's entrance.

"Of course. You don't think I'd take a day off without my boss's permission, do you?"

He gave her a dry look. "Right." Somehow, in spite of Cassie's daredevil driving and all the reasons why he shouldn't be where he was, he was beginning to relax, just as she'd told him to. "You want to tell me where we're going?"

"Nope. Us kidnappers prefer to surprise our victims."

She probably expected him to argue. For some reason he didn't want to. The wicker hamper perfumed the air with the scent of the fried chicken she'd mentioned earlier. He supposed she had some sort of picnic in mind, even though it was November and about fifty degrees outside. He could handle that, silly as the whole business was, if it made her happy. Dallas had plenty of parks, so they ought to reach the one she'd chosen soon.

Gideon didn't even notice when he relaxed and leaned his head back against the seat's headrest.

Cassie hadn't left him. For some crazy reason she'd decided to forgive him, though he'd done nothing at all to earn her forgiveness. Later he would try to understand why. Later.... He realized with some surprise that he was tired. He hadn't slept well while he was gone. It felt surprisingly good not to talk, not even to think, while he watched her maneuver her clunky old car through traffic.

She wasn't really a bad driver, he realized. A bit abrupt, perhaps, and not as patient as he considered wise. But she kept track of the cars around her, and she knew where she was going and how she intended to get there. She simply didn't make the trip the same way he would have.

He inhaled deeply and smelled fried chicken and, more

faintly, paint solvent, a smell he'd grown to associate with
Cassie. Beneath those scents lay the barest whiff of her perfume, a faint, heady blend that made him think of rain and
green, dripping leaves. And beneath that...beneath the perfume, he remembered, was the unique scent of this one
woman, the subtle musk of skin and intimacy. The smell of
Cassie.

His eyes closed. He wanted to be close enough to smell her
again, wanted to press his face into her neck and breathe her
in...he had to apologize first, of course. It was necessary to
clear the air, to communicate. Even if she didn't understand
that he owed her, he knew he did. He had to know what his
obligation entailed, how he could repay her for her generosity
in forgiving him so freely, so foolishly...

When Cassie glanced over at Gideon after adjusting her
speed to that of the traffic on I-20, he was asleep. Even with
his lashes mink dark against his cheeks, his enticing lips
slightly parted, he didn't look vulnerable or boyish. The strong
chin and harsh facial bones proclaimed him very much a man.

He must have been awfully tired, she thought, to doze off
in spite of his preference for being the one behind the wheel.
He must have been...able to trust her.

Her eyes filled. She had to dash the tears away or risk driving with rainbows starring her vision. It was absurd. Absolutely ridiculous, really. She'd loved Gideon forever, lusted
after him for years. She'd *married* him, for goodness sake. So
why should she suddenly think, with a bittersweet ache of
certainty, that it was only now that she really fell in love with
him?

Eight

Gideon slept the seventy minutes it took Cassie to reach her goal. When she slowed down to exit the interstate, he stirred. When he woke fully, glanced around and realized they'd left Dallas altogether, the look on his face was priceless.

"Hi, there," she said cheerfully. "Getting hungry?"

"Where are we?" he demanded.

"Ah," she said, signaling her next turn, "your nap refreshed you. You're back to growling orders."

"Cassie—"

"We're in Absdale, or just outside of it. Be patient just a few minutes longer, okay?"

"I haven't been patient. I've been asleep."

"Close enough. Oh, look—you can see it now!" As the two-lane road wound down a wooded hill, they could see the tidy sprawl of a typical, small, East Texas town. On its outskirts, just off the county road they traveled, was the fair she'd read about.

"Oh, no," he said. "Surely not. Tell me you didn't drag

me away from the office and drive for hours just to go to a two-bit traveling carnival?''

"We have not been driving for hours.''

"Cassie, if you had an urge to ride on roller coasters or something, I would have been glad to take you to Six Flags.''

"Six Flags is fun, but it's not the same. This,'' she told him firmly as she slowed for the turn, "is not just a carnival. It's an old-fashioned country fair. They'll have booths and pigs and rides and blue-ribbon jellies. Where else can you find all that?'' As soon as she'd seen the tiny ad in the paper that morning, she'd known she had to get Gideon to go.

"You want pigs?'' he asked dryly.

"Among other things. I mean—a carnival is sort of like a cut-rate Vegas, isn't it? A tinsel and popcorn version. I don't want candlelight and lies any more than you do, Gideon,'' she said, holding her voice steadier than she could keep her heart. "But I would love some cotton candy and a ride on the Ferris wheel.''

He didn't speak. She sneaked a glance at him before turning onto the dirt track that bisected an empty field, heading to where booths, rides and stock pens spilled out over trampled pastureland. He was watching her steadily in that way he had that tended to wreck her breathing. "You can win something for me by knocking over milk bottles with a tennis ball, and I'll win something for you at the shooting gallery. I'm a very good shot,'' she told him, pleased, in spite of the nerves, with his attention. She could almost taste the sticky sweetness of the cotton candy, too. "Do you want to eat lunch now, or go get sick on some rides first?''

The car bumped down the twin ruts towards the makeshift parking lot. "This is what you really want to do?'' he said at last.

He sounded so dubious, so resigned. She laughed. "You're going to love it.''

They postponed lunch and headed for the livestock pens first, where Cassie cooed over an elaborately groomed black-faced sheep and struck up a conversation with its ten-year-old owner. Upwind of the Herefords was a tent with the jellies Cassie had mentioned, as well as huge yellow squash and all sorts of products from local gardens and kitchens. They got there just in time for the judging of the baked goods. A peach pie baked by a sweet-faced old lady took second prize. Her nephew, a strapping blond fellow with a beard and a lumber-jack's red flannel shirt, beamed when his apple brown Betty took first.

The air was crisp with fall, the crowd was small but festive, and Cassie did, indeed, win a stuffed animal for Gideon at the shooting booth. She insisted he pick out the one he wanted. Somehow he wound up with a brown teddy bear wearing a plaid bow tie.

"So conservative," she said, laughing up at him as the huckster behind the counter handed him his bear. "No pink boa constrictors for you, huh? Come on and buy me a soft drink. I want to ride the Tilt-A-Whirl, and I have to take my pill first."

He had to dodge a woman with a stroller and two toddlers to keep up with her. "What pill? You're not sick, are you?"

"No, and I don't mean to get that way." She stopped in front of the concession stand, where a sign informed them precisely how outrageous the prices were. The air was rich with the smells of caramel, cotton candy and buttered popcorn. "I get motion sickness sometimes," she told him. "Oh, yes. Cotton candy. I need some of that, too."

"You get motion sickness, but you intend to ride the Tilt-A-Whirl—after eating cotton candy," he said as he dug out his wallet. "I suppose you want to go on the Hammer, too?"

"Definitely." The air held the peculiar clarity of autumn, a lucid quality he could taste with every breath he took. The luminous air, though, was nothing compared to the glow in Cassie's eyes as she grinned at him. "And the Spider and that ride with the little chairs that go spinning out at the end of their chains. We can finish up with the Ferris wheel. That's why I'm going to take a pill first, so I can enjoy myself without getting sick."

"By all means," he said dryly. "Take your pill. Take two."

"One's enough." She collected her soda and made him hold the cotton candy while she dug in her huge purse for the motion sickness medicine and dosed herself. "There," she said, and pulled off a wad of sticky pink fluff from the mound on top of the cone he held. Instead of eating it herself, she held it up to his mouth. "Are you having fun, Gideon?" she asked softly. A smile lingered at the corners of her mouth, but her eyes deepened to a serious, mossy gray.

"Yes," he said, surprising himself. "Yes, I am."

"Good." She moved the cotton candy nearer, brushing it across his lower lip. "Open up."

Mesmerized, he obeyed. Hadn't he been following her lead all day? It wasn't so bad, he discovered, to let someone else drive the car, set the pace, choose the destination. Not just this once. Not when that someone had eyes like a mermaid, eyes as deep as the ocean, as changeable as sunlight.

The sweetness she placed in his mouth melted instantly. Along with spun sugar, he tasted memories. He spoke without thinking. "I traveled with a carnival one summer."

Her eyes widened. She took the cotton candy and pulled off a bite for herself. "You did?"

"Yeah. My father worked one of the booths." He shook his head, surprised by both the memory and his willingness to speak of it. "He was supposed to help assemble the rides, actually, but he was a much better huckster than laborer."

Restless, he took her hand in his and started to walk, the teddy bear she'd won for him tucked under his other arm. Where he went didn't matter. He was sampling the corner of the past that the cotton candy had summoned. These memories, he discovered, weren't as unpleasant as some.

"Did you like it?"

"What nine-year-old boy wouldn't think the carnival was cool? There was always plenty to eat and to do. We shared a tiny trailer with this incredibly fat man." Jim Bob Haggerman.

Gideon remembered the name, and the man, with a smile. He recalled how Jim Bob's cigars had stunk up the little silver Airstream trailer, and the awesome sight of the man's mounds and rolls of fat glistening with sweat. Jim Bob had always been sweaty.

He chuckled. "Jim Bob liked to sit around in his underwear, but you couldn't even see his shorts when he sat down. Just stomach, miles and miles of stomach. He said that a man as fat as he was didn't need any clothes to keep warm. He only wore them when he went outside to keep from getting arrested."

"He sounds like quite a character."

He nodded, part of his attention on the past, part on the simple pleasure of holding her hand in his. How many years had it been since he held a woman's hand? "Carnivals are full of characters."

"Were you sorry to leave at the end of the summer?"

"Not really. It was time for school to start, and I was a funny kind of kid. I liked school. It was...dependable." The hours spent at school had also been hours when Gideon was responsible only for himself. He'd cherished that freedom, although he'd felt guilty for wanting time free of taking care of Charlie.

The guilt had been worse later, of course. After the accident. He'd come to terms with it eventually, when he was able to look back with an adult's eyes and see that no little boy should be blamed for occasionally craving time to be a little boy. "Even in a new school," he said, "and I went to plenty of those, it didn't take long to learn what to expect."

"I'm surprised about your dad working as a carnie," she said hesitantly. "I know you didn't have any money when you were in college, but you said that was your aunt's way, that she wanted you to work for what you got. I had the impression, though, that your family used to be well-off."

"'Used to be' is the key phrase." Bitterness burned the back of his throat, a familiar bile. "There was some money, not a huge amount, from my grandfather. By the time I was seven and my mother died, both the money and the family's good name were gone. My father was a wheeler-dealer in the oil business, you see, until people caught on to the fact that he was as slippery as a crooked politician and less reliable. Some of his associates might have overlooked his morals, since they weren't any better equipped themselves, but no one wanted to deal with a crook who turned into a drunk unpredictably.''

They'd wandered into the section devoted to kiddie rides. On his left little airplanes rayed out from a central pole, dipping sedately up and down as they revolved. Two of them held solemn-eyed toddlers who didn't look too sure of the stability of their tiny craft. On his right a merry-go-round blared one of Sousa's marches while its painted steeds rose and fell in their endless, circling dance. One of the riders, a little girl with a dozen braids and a huge grin, held tight to the pole that bisected her crimson horse and shouted to her mother, "Watch me! Look at me!"

Gideon remembered another child, another merry-go-round. How many times that summer, he wondered with a pain so old it was almost comfortable, had he heard those words? *Watch me,* Charlie would call. *Look at me.*

The little girl's words worked a magic he couldn't bring himself to fight. His feet drifted to a stop as his mind drifted into the past, a brown teddy bear in one hand while his other hand held on to Cassie. "The old man who operated the merry-go-round liked to hit the bottle as much as my father did, but he was more consistent about it. A lot of afternoons he'd sneak off to town for a few drinks and leave me to run the thing."

"But you were only nine." She sounded horrified.

He grinned. "Operating a merry-go-round is pretty simple, Cassie. Push forward on the lever and the thing goes. Pull back and it slows and stops."

"You liked running it."

"Yeah. The carnival was okay." Gideon's grin faded. "Of course, my father probably wouldn't have taken the job if we hadn't been locked out of our apartment for not paying the rent. Not that it was much of an apartment—the roaches had won the battle for territory long before we moved in—but there were some things I hated to lose.'' Like the pictures of his mother, and of Charlie. Twenty-seven years later, he hadn't forgiven his father for losing those pictures.

Cassie didn't say anything, but she didn't have to. She was horrified. He could see it in the expression on her face, feel it in the way her hand tightened on his. Perversely he wanted to tell her things that would shock her even more. He knew how cold winter could get when the gas bill went unpaid, and what it was like to get by without water because even that had been shut off. Gideon remembered the heavy weight of darkness when he'd been home at night without lights, phone or food while his father was off on a binge.

Not that they'd been broke all the time. Sometimes they'd stayed in perfectly decent middle-class housing, and a couple of times their place had been downright luxurious. Timothy Wilde had been born charming, and had worked at perfecting his one gift. Since that charm was the only thing he ever put much effort into, he'd made himself into a fairly good con man.

Constant poverty might have been easier to adapt to, though, than their constantly changing fortunes.

"One thing I've never understood is why he didn't just split. Why he kept—'' Gideon almost said *kept us*. The near slip jolted him. A muscle jumped in his jaw as he reined in his tongue, and his thoughts. ''Why he kept me with him. No,'' he told Cassie firmly before she could speak, ''don't say it. Don't tell me that in spite of his flaws he must have loved me. The bastard never really gave a damn about anything but money, which he couldn't hang on to, and his bottle.''

Cassie couldn't speak. She wanted to, but she was afraid that if she tried to speak she'd start crying instead. Gideon would hate that. So she kept her mouth shut and wrapped her arm around him, leaning her head against his shoulder.

After a moment he put his arm around her, too. "She's really having a good time, isn't she?"

It took Cassie a minute to realize he was talking about the little girl on the merry-go-round, who had gained enough confidence to remove one hand from the pole so she could wave madly at her mother. It took her no time at all to understand that he was uncomfortable with all he'd revealed. "She sure is."

"I liked watching the kids when I ran the merry-go-round. They enjoyed themselves so much."

You were just a kid yourself, she wanted to say. But she understood that he hadn't really been a child. Not the way that little girl was, or the way Cassie herself had been. She cleared the wobble out of her throat. "Did I ever tell you about the time I fell off a carousel horse?"

"Come on, Cassie, no one falls off."

"I did. That was the year I wanted to be a cowboy, you see. I was six. Mom had taken Ryan and me to the rodeo a few weeks before, and I was inspired. I could ride with no hands when I was seated, but not so well when my act went on to the next stage. My foot slipped before I even got into standing position, and down I went. I was mortified."

"You could have been killed," he muttered, looking intensely aggravated. "Lord, Cassie, you never have stopped to think, have you? Even when you were little. You launch yourself out into space and wait to see if gravity is for real or just a rumor."

She laughed, delighted with his irritation. He couldn't brood over the past and fret over her at the same time. "Come on," she said, linking her arm through his. "I can't get on the Tilt-A-Whirl yet because my pill hasn't taken effect, so you have time to win me something. I want something big," she warned him as she tugged on his arm, "and really tasteless."

"Cassie." Some new tone in his voice alerted her. His eyes were as dark and wary as those of any wild thing when confronted by kindness. "Why did you bring me here? Why aren't you angry for the way I treated you the night before I left town?''

Love ached. It swelled inside her and hurt. She hadn't known that love could bring a pain so poignant it was almost pleasure. ''I've never been able to hold on to a good mad,'' she told him. ''It just dribbles away after a while.''

She didn't want to tell him the whole truth. Soon after he left town she'd realized two things. First, she had at least accomplished one goal that night. She'd broken through the icy control to the man beneath. Maybe the sheer intensity of his reaction had sent her running like a scared rabbit, but she had broken through. The second thing she'd learned was just as important. She knew now that he was as caught up in the flood tide of passion as she was.

She certainly couldn't tell him the real reason she'd forgiven him. Not yet. He wouldn't want to hear that it was always easy for her to forgive the people she loved.

''Come on,'' she said, grinning up at the tall, brooding man with the teddy bear under his arm. ''Let's go play.''

At three o'clock the next day Gideon sat as his desk, but he wasn't working. Instead, he had his album out again. It lay open to the page he'd added seven years ago, back when he began refining his ideas of how to get the home he wanted.

The woman in the photo wasn't Melissa. He hadn't met her yet at that time. No, at that point he'd settled for a newspaper clipping of a pretty young woman who had written a book about the dying art of homemaking. It wasn't the woman in the picture, pretty and pleasant as she was, that had interested him, of course. It was what she represented.

There were other pictures. Gideon thumbed through the album, pausing on those pages devoted to the dream he thought of as a goal. He'd pulled out the album because he felt so unsettled all day. His longest-held goal seemed strangely distant. He wanted to remind himself of what was important, but he was having trouble concentrating. He kept remembering the

glow in Cassie's eyes when he'd won her a garish purple al-
ligator at the carnival.

The single, perfunctory rap on the door was Mrs. Pittinger's
usual announcement of her intentions. She opened the door
and said, "Your aunt is here."

Gideon felt a pang of alarm. It wasn't like Aunt Eleanor to
show up without calling first, and they would see each other
at her friend's party tomorrow night. Whatever brought her
here today must be urgent. He hurriedly slid his album into
his briefcase to get it out of sight. "Ask her to come in."

His aunt entered, carrying her coat over one arm, her purse
and an envelope-style portfolio in the other. "Good afternoon,
Gideon. I trust you are well?"

She didn't look ill or troubled. But Gideon knew that Eleanor Wilde would greet the Grim Reaper courteously when the
time came, inquiring after his health and family. "I'm fine,
Aunt Eleanor. Is something wrong?"

"Really, you might offer me a seat first." She crossed to
the two armchairs by the window, laid the ivory-colored wool
coat on the back of the chair, then seated herself. She kept the
slim leather portfolio in her lap. "I apologize if my sudden
visit alarmed you, but do sit down so we can talk. There is
no immediate crisis, I assure you, although there is a problem."

Gideon followed and sat slowly. "Is it your health?"

Her cheeks pinkened slightly. "Heavens, no. Though I suppose I am selfish enough to be a bit pleased by your concern.
No, Gideon, I am here about your problem, not one of my
own."

Gideon kept silent and hoped she didn't mean what he
thought she meant.

She opened the leather folder on her lap and pulled something out. "I have here a report prepared by Appleton and
Paine. They are an investigative service recommended to me
by—"

"Good God." He shoved to his feet. "I can't believe this."

"Calm yourself, Gideon. It will do no good to stamp around

the room cursing. If you wish to disagree with me, do me the courtesy of hearing me out, first.''

"If you're going to tell me that you had Cassie investigated by some scuzzball P.I. firm, I don't want to hear about it.''

"Appleton and Paine are rather too expensive to be called scuzzballs," she said dryly. She stood and held out the report with its neat, white label fixed to the dark blue folder. When he made no move to take it from her, she sighed and walked to his desk. "It isn't like you to imitate an ostrich, but I understand that you find the idea of probing Cassandra's past distasteful. Really, though, if she has nothing to hide, what can it hurt?" She laid the report on his desk.

"There's the matter of her privacy." He ran a hand over his hair. "I knew you were unhappy about my marriage, but I thought that was because I'd acted so rashly. I had no idea your antipathy for Cassie went this far."

"I have no antipathy for Cassandra," she said sharply. "I find some of her behavior a bit distasteful, perhaps, but I assure you I have conceived no violent animus for the girl. I don't pretend to be entirely objective, however. She did manipulate you into marrying her while you were drunk."

"The marriage was my idea, not hers. I've told you that." Anger twisted together in his gut with a hollow, lost feeling. Aunt Eleanor was the only relative he had left. Her attack on Cassie confused him as much as it angered him. "I had to talk her into it."

"Certainly you are convinced it was your idea. She is leading you around by the…hormones. That is quite obvious to another woman, although I suppose I shouldn't be surprised you can't see it yourself."

"You've always told me that only a weakling blames his behavior on other people, on circumstances or on biology. Why are you blaming Cassie for my choices?"

"Whatever blame falls on you for your part in this absurd marriage, it does not exonerate her from her own guilt." She walked back to the chairs and retrieved her purse and the now-empty portfolio. Eleanor Wilde's stride was an anomaly. She moved with the smooth confidence of youth, a sharp contrast to the aging fragility of her skin and the delicate bone structure that made her look easily crushed. "Read the report, Gideon."

"I've known Cassie for more than half her life. That damned report can't possibly tell me anything that's any of my business."

"No?" The arch of her brows was a subtle thing. "Then you already know all about the men in her life?" With a minute shift of tone, her voice altered from dispassionate to mocking as she moved toward the door. "I congratulate you. Few husbands are so well informed, or so tolerant. Not that I would presume to suggest that she slept with *all* of the men she's gone out with. That would be…excessive, wouldn't it? Even for a creature as impulsive and mercurial as your Cassandra." She laid her hand on the doorknob, and half turned to deliver one parting blow in a voice as soft and well groomed as her white hair and ivory wool dress. "But there were a great many men, Gideon."

He said nothing, absolutely nothing.

"I'll see you at Barbara's party tomorrow night," she said in exactly the same tone of voice. Then she left, shutting the door behind her with a quiet click.

Gideon stared at the closed door for several moments. He had a paper shredder in his office, right next to the desk. That's what he should do with his aunt's damned report, he thought savagely. Shred it sight unseen. It didn't matter, couldn't matter, what men had been in her past. She was his now.

Wasn't she?

Four hours later, when Gideon left the office, the blue cover of the report was in his briefcase next to the scuffed old album. That night he went straight to his bedroom after dinner and proved both himself and his aunt correct. He had been right when he'd said he had no business reading the report. She had been right when she'd left it on his desk, confident that she knew which buttons to push, how to make it impossible for him to ignore the serpent's gift she'd brought him.

It didn't make for soothing bedtime reading.

* * *

Something was wrong. By the time Cassie stepped from the bathtub the next evening, she knew something was wrong just as certainly as she knew that the chill she felt didn't come from the perfectly heated bathroom. No, she thought as she toweled off, the cold she felt came from deep inside, from the place that only Gideon reached.

Cassie had felt strengthened and hopeful after their time at the fair. Gideon had opened up to her, after all. He'd talked about important things, about his childhood and his father. So maybe his confidences had left him feeling a little too exposed and he'd hidden himself away in his room the last two nights. She hadn't pushed, not wanting to crowd him or panic him.

At least, she hadn't wanted to *then*. But she'd given him enough time. Tonight—either at the party or later—she meant to drive him crazy.

She tossed the wet towel over the shower curtain rod and stepped into what might be called a pair of panties: a scrap of crimson satin held in place by stretchy black lace. It was quite lusciously wicked, and the color was an exact match for the shocking red dress that hung on the back of the door.

It didn't take long to blow dry her hair. When she finished, she paused, studying her image in the mirror.

She had, she thought, a nice, round little bottom and good legs, and hips were supposed to be more curvy than bony. But her breasts—if only her breasts were bigger. Maybe then the annoying flutter of nerves in the pit of her stomach would die down. Maybe then she'd be more confident, better able to contemplate the night ahead.

Something had happened yesterday after she'd left work, something that turned Gideon cold again. He hadn't been cold at breakfast that day. He'd hinted that he had plans for that night, plans for her. Delicious little prickles danced over her skin at the memory. A smile tipped her mouth up in spite of her jangling nerves as she thought about the way he'd looked at her. Yet last night at supper he'd been distant again, pre-occupied. This morning—oh, this morning he'd been in a rage.

Probably, she thought as she went to work on her face, outlining her eyes with kohl and her lips with crimson, he hadn't thought she knew how angry he was. But what some-one else might have taken for calm, she knew was the icy control imposed on a reckless temper.

Very likely it had something to do with work, she assured herself as she smudged shadow on her eyelids and darkened her eyebrows. Probably his mood had nothing to do with her.

She wished she believed that. If she'd been able to swallow her doubts, maybe she could have swallowed some supper earlier, too.

He *ought* to tell her what was bothering him, of course. He should trust her enough to tell her anything, but Cassie was realist enough to recognize that it would take a while to get him used to confiding in her.

She reached for the dress she'd found that afternoon in a boutique called Rethreads, a fascinating little store Jaya knew about. Rethreads sold second-hand but first-class designer eve-ning wear, everything from cocktail dresses to ankle-length formals to intriguingly oddball outfits that defied classification. Their prices were still pretty outrageous, in Cassie's opinion. But for tonight's party she'd wanted something special. Not just because she wanted to boost her confidence in front of Gideon's aunt, his aunt's friend and their wealthy acquaintances, either.

Lord knows, she thought as she shimmied into the delicate silk, *I'm not wearing this particular dress for those people.* She tied the wraparound skirt at the waist, smoothed it down and looked in the mirror again.

Her hair—well, there was no reasoning with hair like hers. Cassie had learned years ago to let it have its way. But her dress and her makeup...she smiled as she studied the effect. Cassie seldom bothered with more than a hit-or-miss approach to cosmetics. But once in a while she enjoyed playing dress up, and on occasions like tonight she liked to pull out all the stops.

She contemplated the glamorous woman in the mirror with a satisfied nod. That person wasn't her, of course. She was an illusion, a testimonial to Cassie's artistic ability. But she looked damned good. The dress made the most of what Cassie considered her assets—her legs and her rear end. It was, maybe, a bit obvious, but Cassie wasn't feeling patient. The style consisted of a few wisps of lipstick red silk held up at the right shoulder by a rhinestone clasp. Cassie's left shoulder was bare, as was most of her right leg, because of the drape of the wraparound skirt. She reminded herself to be careful that the slippery silk didn't slip around too much.

In the store the dress had reminded Cassie of Tinkerbell...sort of. This dress belonged to an 'adults only' version, one who intended to seduce her Peter Pan.

Just like Cassie intended to seduce her husband tonight.

Oh, boy. She rested her hand just below her waist where nerves twisted, inhaled slowly, and reminded herself of the decision she'd made while Gideon was gone over the weekend. It was a logical decision, she assured herself, just as logical as her original goal of staying out of his bed had been. She had, after all, met her goals...mostly. They'd been married for two weeks and one day now, so she *had* waited. Just not very long. But flexibility was important, wasn't it? And Gideon had opened up to her at the fair, so he was starting to trust her. Trust...that was a reasonable goal.

She certainly wasn't going to seduce Gideon just because she couldn't sleep at night for wanting him, or because when he looked at her in that man-woman way she wanted to strip then and there and offer herself to him...or because her body hungered for his while her soul ached for the combination of shelter and storm his arms could provide.

Well, not just for those reasons, anyway. She was *not* letting him get away with turning cold again. With another little nod to encourage herself, Cassie reached for the doorknob.

* * *

Gideon was in a savage temper. He slid back the raw silk cuff of his evening jacket so he could glance at his watch again. What the hell was keeping her? Cassie wasn't one of those women who primped forever. She got ready for work every morning almost as quickly as he did.

Not that his temper had anything to do with whether or not they were late to Barbara Johnson's blasted party. He was in no mood to see his aunt, not with the contents of her "gift" making a lump in his middle like a snake's meal—swallowed but undigested. He thought of the report in its businesslike blue folder that he'd left on the desk in his bedroom, and scowled.

It didn't matter, he reminded himself for the hundredth time. How many men she'd gone out with, even how many of those men she'd gone to bed with, had little to do with their relationship now. He *knew* that, dammit. So it didn't matter whether he believed the report or not.

Gideon crossed to the bar with a muttered curse about time, parties and women in general. He poured himself a shot of Scotch. He would relax, dammit. There was no logical reason for him to be upset. He'd known that Cassie dated a lot. Ryan had joked about his sister's habit of skipping lightly through the vast numbers of Dallas's eligible male population. And Gideon wasn't the sort of man who held to one standard for his own behavior while expecting something different from the women he went out with.

At least, he never had been before.

But now, he thought with bewildered anger, I know their names. It made a difference, knowing the names of the men Cassie had dated over the past few years. Now he had descriptions for some of them. Occupations. He knew approximately when they'd dated Cassie, whether they still saw her...everything but whether or not Cassie had been to bed with them.

Or *which* of them, specifically, she'd been to bed with. The report didn't say, although it implied...there was that man she called Mo. The one he'd seen her with the day she'd moved into his apartment. Unlike most of the men she'd dated, she and this Moses Armstrong had been close for a long time. Years.

It doesn't matter, he told himself, and tossed the Scotch down his throat, letting it burn, burn, burn going down. Then he heard his name and turned.

She wore red. And not enough of it.

His gaze started at the strappy sandals that let her red-tipped toes peek out, slid up the creamy skin of her legs to where her red shout of a dress finally began, traveled over curves veiled in red silk to pause at pale shoulders scattered with freckles, then stopped. Her face—Lord, but she looked different. With her eyes all sultry dark and her lips pouting red, she looked like an exotic stranger. Shaken, he looked again at her silk-draped body and thought suddenly of another night. Another red dress.

Gideon had been twenty-six on that January second, and still celebrating New Year's in the way every bachelor wants to—with a lovely and eager lady. He had no idea, now, what the woman's name had been, though he did recall that it had been she, not he, who removed her bra. Not that he'd objected.

Then his doorbell had rung.

He'd almost let it go unanswered. Who could it be, after all, at that hour on a holiday weekend? But the demon that had driven him to prosper in business wouldn't let him ignore it for long. He'd pried his reluctant body away from the half-naked woman on the couch and opened the damned door.

Cassie had worn red that night. And precious little of it.

"Hell," he said now, and slammed his glass down on the bar. "You are not wearing that outfit."

Her chin came up, but her eyes blinked furiously. "What's wrong with it?"

"Nothing," he growled. "Not a damned thing. It's gorgeous. You're gorgeous. But too much of you—" he patted the air vaguely with his hands "—shows."

She looked down at herself and stretched out one leg. The dress gaped open, revealing lots of pale, firm thigh, and he realized she wasn't wearing any panty hose. That was bare skin he was looking at....

"No," she said thoughtfully, "I don't think there's too much showing. I think it's about right." She looked up and smiled.

"Hell," he said again, with feeling. "Let's go."

She's wearing perfume, he thought several minutes later as he closed the car door, shutting them up together in the quiet, dark space of his Porsche. Cassie never wore perfume, but she was tonight. He felt awkward, as if he were with a stranger, the same stranger who'd shown up at his apartment one night eight years ago in a red tease of a dress when he was already aroused. The stranger who had until then been a girl to him, not a woman...a woman he'd damned near made love to that long-ago night, there on the floor by his front door, while the woman he'd fondled earlier waited on the couch.

Gideon endured the wave of self-disgust that rolled over him. He'd come too close, eight years ago, to losing his mind along with his control. But on that other night he hadn't had an inkling of what was possible with this woman. Tonight he was prepared. It wouldn't happen again.

"I'm a little nervous," the Scarlet Woman beside him said.

He shot her a skeptical glance. Her dress had ridden up when she'd sat down, and the black coat she'd shrugged into before they'd left was unfastened, hanging open in front. Her lovely, bare legs stretched out in front of her. "I can't believe you're wearing that in November, for God's sake." Aggravated, he turned up the heater.

"Gideon, I don't know any of these people."

"Since when has that bothered you? Besides, Barbara's crowd is into art. You'll probably have some acquaintances in common." He accelerated smoothly into the traffic along the main artery that led to the exclusive new development outside of Dallas where his aunt's friend had recently built her new home. He was not going to look at Cassie's legs, he promised himself, not while he was driving. "You don't exactly hold people at a distance." There would be plenty of men at the party who would be glad to make her welcome. His fingers tightened on the steering wheel.

She crossed her legs. The silk slipped farther up her thigh. "Tonight is different."

Damn. He could have kept his promise if she hadn't moved. But the way that red silk slithered around...no man could help looking.

Every man at the party would be looking. He discovered that he didn't want to share even that much of her, and abruptly, with a hollow feeling in his stomach, he understood why he couldn't get that damned report out of his mind. Why it had thrown him into an emotional whirlpool that kept sucking him down.

Not because he believed the promiscuity the report hinted at. No, in spite of logic and the investigator's carefully compiled facts and even Cassie's damned slippery dress and painted face tonight, he didn't believe it. That's what he couldn't handle. He was afraid that if he walked in on a hot clinch between Cassie and another man, he'd stand there shaking his head, disbelieving what he saw. And this inability, this unwilled, insane reliance on what he felt instead of what reason told him was true, terrified him.

"Gideon, promise me you'll stay with me at the party and not hide in the corner discussing business or something."

He could ask. Cassie, sweet, feckless Cassie, would probably tell him the truth about her past romantic adventures...if he asked. And he'd believe it. He would, he thought with a bolt of pure fear, believe whatever she chose to tell him. "You'll make 'friends' fast enough," he snarled, "if you sit down in that dress and treat everyone to the same view you're giving me."

She tipped her pointed chin up and looked at him out of haughty, irritated eyes. "I may just climb on the dining room table and do a striptease. Do you think your aunt's friends would be entertained?"

They drove the rest of the way in silence.

Nine

The house where the party was being held was very new, set in a quarter acre of freshly landscaped dirt. The faint whiff of the stables in the air reminded Cassie of what Emma Pittinger had told her about Barbara Johnson—she came from old money and liked to keep young men and horses around.

Inside, the walls were white, the floor was tiled and the furniture looked more like sculpture than something to sit on. Here and there a painting or other objet d'art hung in lonely splendor on one of those white walls, commanding attention.

Cassie knew it was all very elegant, even effective. She just didn't like it. Less than five minutes after entering the house, she knew she wasn't going to like her hostess, either. Barbara Johnson was small and dark-haired and beautifully groomed except for her fingernails, which were brutally short and unpolished. Her eyes were as quick and remote as a lizard's, and they darted between Cassie and Gideon after she let her little bombshell fall.

Gideon sucked in his breath. Cassie stood with him and their hostess in full view of the large living area where guests milled around. *Did they know?* Cassie wondered sickly. Did they all know that this woman had invited Gideon's former fiancée to the party that was supposed to honor his new marriage?

Gideon spoke. "Get Cassie's coat back from the maid you just passed it to. We're leaving."

"Well, really, Gideon, what did you expect me to do?" Barbara Johnson's dark eyes flicked from Cassie to Gideon and back as lightly as a dragonfly skims the surface of a pond. "You know that Melissa's mother is married to one of my cousins. Did you think I should cut the connection on your behalf?" She shook her head and slid her arm through one of Cassie's, effectively pinning her in place while still talking to Gideon. "Don't be childish, dear. Your sudden marriage was quite a blow to Melissa. You owe it to her to help her put a good face on things." She glanced at Cassie with a cool smile. "Doesn't he, dear?"

Gideon spoke before Cassie could. "I owe her nothing. *She* broke the engagement."

"But you didn't mourn. So tactless, not to pine for a few months, at least."

Gideon's mouth thinned to a hard line. He grabbed Cassie's other arm and told her, "Come on. With or without your coat, we're leaving."

If he had asked what she wanted—if she hadn't still been so bloody mad at him for his comments about her dress—if he'd just looked at her, instead of tugging on her arm as if she were a toy he was arguing over, Cassie would never have said it. "I don't think so."

"What?" His eyes, hot with anger, swung to her. "What did you say?"

"We're already here," she said in a deliberately reasonable voice, enjoying the open flash of his temper. He wasn't cold now. "It's going to look peculiar if we turn around and leave."

"Exactly," Barbara Johnson said. "And, Gideon, you wouldn't want everyone to think you were too upset—or

guilty—to face Melissa, would you? There will be a few suspicious souls who assume that your sudden marriage indicates
a very *close* prior relationship with Cassandra, one that Melissa took objection to. But don't worry, dear, I'll take good
care of your little wife.''

"You know," Cassie said, gently detaching her arm from
her hostess's, "I really prefer to be called Cassie. And I'm not
crazy about being called Gideon's little wife. It sounds kind
of patronizing, doesn't it?" She smiled sweetly. "Don't
worry. I'll take good care of myself."

"You've got problems, dear," Barbara Johnson told her
friend.

"Yes." Eleanor Wilde watched as Gideon and his new
bride greeted and were greeted out in the crowded living area.
She sipped at her wine. "I'm surprised he didn't turn around
and leave."

"He wanted to. *She* didn't. You can see which of them got
what they wanted." Barbara slanted her a long look. "She's
not the bit of fluff you described to me, Eleanor."

Eleanor felt a little tremor somewhere deep inside. It was
too late for doubts, however. The detective was already acting
on the rest of his instructions. "She's apparently quite good
at getting what she wants, but the skill has more to do with
sex than intelligence. Instinct and sex."

"Are you sure?"

"Just look at her." Eleanor lifted her glass slightly. Gideon's simple-minded little wife had been charming Barbara's
newest boy-toy. Now she flirted with Amos Bergman, a skinny
old man with pots of money and a lecher's appreciation for a
pretty woman in a skimpy dress. Gideon's blank expression
told his aunt how sorely he found his restraint tested.

Eleanor's nerves steadied as she watched. Trouble was definitely brewing, and the foolish little tart seemed to be courting
it, actively aiding Eleanor's design. She could almost feel
sorry for the creature. "Look at how she's dressed. Is that a

subtle woman, a complex mind? I don't think so." No, Eleanor wasn't wrong. She couldn't afford to be.

At first Cassie just meant to be friendly. Really. She thought that even in his present mood, Gideon couldn't take offense if she joked with a boy who had probably only started shaving last week or flirted mildly with a beanpole of a man old enough to be her grandfather. It kept her from scanning the crowd for Melissa, it relaxed the boy, and it delighted the old man.

Wrong again. After making some excuse to Mr. Bergman, Gideon drew her away. Before anyone else could descend on them, he bent and said pleasantly, in a voice too low for others to hear, "If you're determined to make a fool out of yourself tonight, go right ahead. I won't stay to watch, however, so you'll have to get one of your admirers to bring you home—after you're through entertaining everyone."

"Oh, good grief, Gideon, I was just giving an old man a little attention."

"You left him with the impression you were ready to give him something, all right."

She scowled. A touch of jealousy was, in her opinion, like a bit of flirtation or a pinch of vanity—one of life's seasonings. But this was more than a touch. "That was an ugly thing to say."

"Listen to me." The vicious edge to his voice contradicted the way he held her shoulders and bent over her as if he were whispering sweet things in her ear. "You wanted to stay at the party. We're here. So maybe you could try to act a little more like my wife and a little less like the scheming slut my aunt has probably convinced half these people you are."

The shock of hurt flashed through her, quickly followed by a healthy jolt of fury. "I'm acting like exactly who and what I am. If you don't like it, why not see if you can patch things up with Melissa? She's around here somewhere, according to that reptile who invited us." She pulled on the arm he still held.

"Dammit, Cassie, calm down or you'll—"

"Make a scene?" She stuck her face in his. "I'm sure your former fiancée wouldn't dream of making waves in public, but I like waves. Big, loud, noisy waves."

He drew back. "I don't." And with that, he walked away.

He didn't leave. Oh, no. Keeping track of him wasn't easy, not when Cassie had to flirt madly with everything male that came within range in order to show her fool of a husband the difference between simple friendliness and the sort of behavior he'd accused her of. No, it wasn't easy, but she managed.

He was so blasted gorgeous tonight, in his stark black jacket and crisp white shirt. It made her furious. While she laughed at a young Adonis who thought he was charming her because she let him talk about himself, she watched Gideon over the rim of her champagne glass. The dark-haired woman next to him had her hand on his sleeve. Cassie's eyes narrowed.

That sleeve was silk. No one but her should know that, because the jacket, like Gideon's hair, like his eyes, was as black as midnight, its fire hidden. You had to touch that jacket to know what it was, and Cassie didn't want anyone else touching it. Gideon might be an arrogant fool who needed taking down a few pegs, but he was *her* arrogant fool.

When the young man she'd been flirting with interrupted his monologue to ask her what was wrong, she blinked twice before she remembered his existence. Then she smiled brilliantly and told him she needed more champagne.

Gideon watched her. It was both easy and terribly hard, watching Cassie. She was impossible to miss, like a brightly colored tropical fish in a tankful of minnows, a splash of life more vivid than any of Barbara's carefully spotlighted paintings. Her hair alone drew the eye. Then there was the way she had of moving, a grace as natural as the glide of a fish through the water…or that of a mermaid at home in the sea. Veil that grace in a flutter of red silk hot enough to set off the smoke detectors, and…he downed the rest of his drink. The 'heat detectors' in the men she went near were going off, all right.

She was determined to drive him crazy. He knew it and still

he felt his sanity slipping. Had he thought that the madness that was Cassie was all sweetness and the clean burn of desire? He was learning differently tonight.

The woman beside him murmured something about a play she'd seen. He answered automatically, watching as Cassie slipped, an enticing little fish, from one man to the next. How many men, he wondered, feeling the pressure building inside, did she require in order to punish him properly?

He'd behaved badly. From the moment they arrived—no, from the moment he'd seen her in that damned, dangerous dress of hers, he'd behaved badly. He knew it, and if she'd ease up for a minute, just long enough for him to get himself back under control, he would go to her and apologize. Just as soon as he could be sure he wasn't going to throw her to the floor and take her like a beast in rut.

He watched as, across the room, Cassie beamed up at the heir to a trucking fortune, a brawny man with two ex-wives who happened to lack a mistress at the moment. He saw the trucker put his hand on her arm.

The pressure mounted impossibly higher.

"She's stunning, Gideon."

It wasn't a voice he'd been expecting. He should have, of course. He'd been warned. Slowly Gideon turned and looked at his ex-fiancée.

"We need to talk," Melissa said. "Privately."

Cassie glanced across the room and saw the tall blonde in the ice blue dress talking to Gideon. She went as still as a trapped rabbit...or a stalking cat. Even though she couldn't see the woman's face, she knew who it was.

When the handsome young man she'd sent after some champagne returned with her glass, she thanked him absently. "I have something I need to do," she told him, and without looking back she slipped away through the crowd.

Making Gideon suffer was all very well, but Cassie hoped she wasn't a fool. She wasn't about to stay away while the husband she'd worked hard to enrage slipped off for a tête-à-tête with the woman he'd wanted to marry instead of her.

Unfortunately an art critic slowed her down. By the time she reached the place where she'd seen Gideon and Melissa, they were gone.

The first door Cassie looked behind revealed a library. The couple who had appropriated the room and the couch it contained didn't appreciate her intrusion. That was tough. She was not leaving Gideon alone in some isolated room with the Icicle. Who knew but what the woman might start to melt?

She located a bathroom, the dining room, a bedroom that was being used as a combination cloak room and powder room for the ladies and the kitchen. No sign of either Gideon or Melissa. They must have gone back to the living area while she was searching. Yet when she got back there she still couldn't spot either of them.

The first fingers of panic skittered up her spine. The only places left to look were outside and upstairs. Outside might appeal to an earthworm—the grounds were mostly still dirt, with leafless twigs stuck here and there, waiting on spring—except that it was supposed to drop to nearly freezing tonight. Which left the upstairs. Upstairs, where all the bedrooms were.

Gideon had drawn Melissa to the shadowy end of the porch, but light from the nearby window still fell softly on her long hair. Her hair, Gideon thought, was the same soft, shining blond it had always been. Her features were still as lovely and composed as the first soft snowfall of winter, and she'd neither gained nor lost any weight…yet something was different about her. Gideon frowned, trying to understand. "All right," he said shortly. "We've got the privacy you wanted."

"I'm freezing," she complained. The afghan he'd grabbed on their way out the door for her to drape, shawllike, around her shoulders wasn't enough protection from the plummeting temperatures.

It wasn't exactly the sort of fashion accessory Melissa usually selected, either. Gideon smiled slightly. "Sorry. But I don't want this to look like an assignation, and the porch seemed like the only place that offered both privacy and a lack of—well, call it romantic opportunity.''

The look she slanted him was equal parts irritation and pride. ''I hope no one would think I would stoop to an assignation with a newly married man. At least—'' humor touched her voice ''—not dressed like this.'' She pulled the afghan more firmly around her.

Neither the humor nor the pride was anything new. He'd known Melissa possessed both, though he would have said the latter outweighed the former. Yet something was different. ''Then tell me what you needed to say, so we can go inside again.''

She looked down. ''This isn't easy. I wanted...I'm sorry, Gideon. I think I'll always regret the way I ended things between us, waiting so late and then not having the courage to tell you in person.''

It was the genuine feeling in her voice more than the apology itself that hit him hardest, and for a moment he felt it all again—the raw, bewildering pain of rejection. ''If you're trying to say you want to get back together,'' he began, his voice harsh, ''it's a little late.''

''No.'' Her chin went up. ''I'm sorry for the way I ended things, not for ending them.''

As he stared at the pretty mouth he'd kissed any number of times, the lips now tight with defiance, he began to understand. It wasn't Melissa who was different. It was him.

He didn't want her anymore. She was the very image of the wife he'd dreamed of for years, yet he didn't want her at all. ''Why?'' he asked softly. ''I need to know that one thing, Melissa. Why did you decide you couldn't marry me?''

''Because I didn't love you. That, in the end, turned out to be even more important than the fact that you didn't love me. I thought,'' she said, almost to herself, ''that what I felt might be love. I wanted it to be. It would have pleased my parents, and you—'' Her laugh held a touch of bitterness. ''You would have liked having me in love with you, wouldn't you, Gideon?

It would have been so convenient, made it even easier to control me.''

He frowned. ''I didn't try to control you.''

''You try to control everything and everyone.'' She sighed. ''Oh, I didn't ask you to speak with me so we could quarrel. I wanted to apologize, to give you a chance to say the things you needed to say. Maybe,'' she said, ''I even hoped we might be friends, eventually.''

Cassie, he thought, would never sidestep a quarrel. No, she'd jump right into whatever argument offered itself, both feet, no holding back. ''Maybe we will,'' he said, and as he did, he realized he would never be able to tuck Cassie back into the safe, tidy compartment of ''friend'' again.

''Gideon? You look…'' Her voice trailed off. She shivered.

He made himself smile at the woman he'd planned to marry. The safe, sane, stable woman who had fit so perfectly into the life he'd worked toward for years. ''Go on inside,'' he told her. ''I'll be along in a minute.''

Gideon watched his former fiancée walk away. His plans, the dreams he'd held for so long, were in ruins. He didn't want Melissa, and he was deathly afraid the change was permanent, all-encompassing. He was no longer able to want the sort of woman he needed to make his dream a reality.

There was only one reason for his transformation, and only one person to blame.

And, he thought, anger clouding his mind and darkening his face, he was going to go find her. Right now.

Gideon would be embarrassed, Cassie told herself, her heart thumping far more than a single flight of stairs could account for, as she started down the second floor hall. Embarrassed and maybe defensive. He would know how sordid it looked for her to find him alone with Melissa in a bedroom. But Cassie trusted Gideon. She knew he wouldn't—well, he just *wouldn't*. Yet who could say what Melissa might do? Cassie could almost feel some sympathy for the foolish woman who'd let Gideon go and now was probably desperate to get him

back, desperate enough to lure him off to some bedroom
and…embarrass him.

Almost.

The first room was empty. Completely. Apparently her hostess hadn't gotten around to furnishing everything yet. Cassie
moved along to the next door on the left, her hands clammy.
She was certain she wouldn't see anything terrible behind that
door, nothing that would change her life or break her heart—
almost completely one hundred percent certain. She trusted
Gideon. She…

Her damp palm slipped a little on the knob as she turned
it, slowly.

The room was dark. Her heart in her throat, she fumbled
along the wall until her fingers found the switch. She turned
it on.

And someone grabbed her from behind.

She squeaked. The arm was hard, and the body it drew her
up against was male and tall and firm, but it never occurred
to her it might be Gideon. It *wasn't* Gideon, didn't feel like
him, didn't smell like him—didn't make her pulse jackhammer
in her veins the way he did.

No, this man felt like a jerk and smelled like a drunk. She
pried at the arm wrapped around her waist while searching the
room in front of her with anxious eyes.

"Hey, sweetie," bourbon-breath whispered into the side of
her face while his free hand tried to take a trip up from her
waist. "This was a good idea. You should've told me yourself
what you had in mind, though. Sometimes Barbara gets pos-
sessive."

She slapped at his wandering hand. Empty, she thought,
short of breath from being squeezed around the middle. The
bedroom in front of her was empty, of people if not of furniture. "Let me go, you idiot. I'm looking for my husband."

He chuckled. "Sure you are, sweetie. That's why you've
been sending me those come-on looks all evening, right? Because you're looking for your husband. And that's why you
had Barbara tell me to follow you up—"

He went flying. Backward. Since his arm still banded her middle, so did she. Only he kept on going while another arm—stronger, harder and infinitely more welcome—grabbed her and jerked her out of bourbon-breath's unwanted embrace before the jerk collided, hard, with the wall.

Her admirer, she saw with surprise, was the boy she'd thought was barely old enough to shave, much less drink bourbon and manhandle women. He sprawled up against the wall Gideon had thrown him into, looking confused.

As for her rescuer... "Good grief," she said, breathless, rubbing her middle. That had gotten a little rough. "You might be more careful when you use me to play tug-of-war, Gideon."

The elegance of Gideon's black jacket was undisturbed, unwrinkled. His conservatively striped silk tie hung neatly from the knot he'd put in it before they'd left the apartment. His dark hair remained sleek and unruffled—and his legs were spread like a back-street fighter's, knees flexed and ready. His fists were clenched, and his jaw was set like granite. Fire and ice burned together in his eyes as he looked down at the man he'd pulled off his wife. "Leave," he said, his voice clipped. "Quickly. Before I kick you to those stairs and down them. And tell Barbara to stop the games before someone gets hurt. Because it might be her."

Cassie shivered, because she almost believed that Gideon would do just that. She put her hand on his arm. "Gideon—"

He shook her off. "Shut up."

She frowned at him.

The man on the floor was none too steady, but he was quick. He scrambled away backward like a spider. Once he was out of immediate range he pushed to his feet and escaped.

"Well," Cassie said. Little quivers shook her deep inside, the aftermath of a fear she hadn't wanted to feel when bourbon-breath grabbed her. She scowled hard to try and keep those stupid quivers stuffed way down. "I guess you heard what he said about Barbara sending him after me, but you should know I didn't—"

"Shut up." He took her wrist and pulled her into the bedroom she'd been checking when the young gorilla seized her.

She sputtered. "I am not going to put up with—stop that right now," she told him, pulling against his grip as he closed the door. "If you expect me to be grateful for this kind of rough treatment, you are way off base. You weren't really rescuing me, anyway—you were just claiming me, like a little boy who sees another kid with his baseball."

"Damn right." He leaned his back up against the door. "There's no lock on the door, so we'll have to stay right here where I can block it with my weight."

"What the—"

He pulled on the wrist he held. She thumped up against him.

He was solid and big and warm even through the layers of clothes he wore, and the fires of hell—or maybe heaven— burned in his dark, dark eyes. He stared down at her for a second. Then his mouth crushed down on hers.

Here was hunger…hers. She sagged against him, seduced by the wildfire song of her blood calling to his, by the flavor of Scotch, passion and Gideon. He couldn't seem to taste enough of her fast enough to stem the fire raging in him. He tried, beginning with her mouth. Apparently his lips, tongue and teeth all needed to sample her, but couldn't linger. He raced over her cheeks and down her throat. The moan that rose from her depths must have pleased him. His hands slid to her bottom and clutched her tightly to him.

"I didn't—" She could hardly get the words out, could hardly find words for the pleasure humming through her. "Gideon, in spite of how it looked, I didn't want that moron to follow me."

"You think I don't know that?" His voice was savage, hardly less angry than when he'd sent the other man crawling away backward. He nipped her bottom lip just hard enough to sting. "It doesn't help. Knowing I can't believe what I see doesn't help." Then he licked the tiny sore he'd inflicted.

Her knees quit on her. She clutched at his arms to keep from sliding to the floor. "Gideon—?"

"I have to have you." His hand, big, warm and welcome, slid up to cover one breast.

Her heart went crazy. "We can't—not here," she managed to say. Not in the house of a woman who'd played a nasty trick on them both, not in the middle of a party, not when the door didn't even have a lock on it. *But there's a bed,* the ache inside her whispered. Only a few steps away. A big, wide bed.

"I'm leaning on the door. No one can get in," he told her, nuzzling her neck, propping her up against him with one hand while his other one abandoned her breast for her shoulder. "And I have to look at what you've been taunting me with. You'll let me," he said in a voice thick with hunger. His hand fumbled with the clasp that held her dress up. "We've both known that for days, that you'd let me have anything I wanted, and—God! I'm only human, Cassie. I have to have some of you. Now."

She would have hit him for his assumptions, if she hadn't already melted. What defense did she have against him or herself when his passion was so honest, so open? She might at least have tried to protest his arrogance if her body hadn't already made its own decision, arching her chest in a mute offering just as the material of her dress fell away from her breasts.

He made a sound, a low, desperate sound, as he stared at her. His hand rose slowly to touch one soft mound, to shape and cup it for his pleasure, then he bent and fastened his mouth on her.

Cassie expected the heat, the pure, carnal pleasure of his mouth tugging at her nipple. She even expected the pleasure to be different, stronger and richer than anything she'd ever felt before, because this was Gideon. She knew there would be lightning and the fire he drew from her so effortlessly. Yet she wasn't prepared for any of it. How could she have been ready to have the world spin away, leaving only sensation— fear and pleasure and a need so fierce she didn't know whether it was his or hers, or if their hunger had somehow merged into a force neither could wholly claim?

Gideon wasn't ready. How could he have been ready for the sound she made, low in her throat, when he sucked at her breast? How could he have been ready for feelings so huge they would surely swallow him, were already devouring him, leaving only, and barely, enough control to keep from hurting her? Yet he couldn't take what he thought he'd die without. Even though, with every twist of her body, she begged him to.

He would take what he could, though. Ragged with a need he couldn't deny or sate, gentle with his hands, he turned her in his arms, keeping his back firmly against the door to guarantee their privacy. She protested. He ignored it, shifting her until he had her positioned just right, her back to his front, with his leg between hers lifting her slightly. She tried to move, to turn, but he held her in place. "Let me," he breathed. "It has to be this way."

Briefly he indulged the rage of heat in his blood by rubbing his groin against her soft flesh. It felt good—dangerously, impossibly good, and he'd no desire to go downstairs with evidence of his arousal, like a thirteen-year-old who'd gotten carried away watching dirty movies. So he abandoned his own stimulation for hers.

Desperate for the feel of her, he slid his hand up her leg, stroking and savoring the creamy skin he'd been craving all evening, pressing kisses into the side of her neck. The hitch in her breath delighted him, but he couldn't delay for long before he had to uncover more of what had been hidden. He pushed up the red silk that had teased him so sorely. When he saw more red silk—a tiny swatch of it banded in black lace—he groaned in an agony of pleasure and frustration.

Cassie didn't want to be like this—helpless, unable to touch him and so needy she hurt. Yet she didn't want to move, because his hand now cupped her right where she hurt and she had, absolutely had, to have his touch.

She felt his chest heave with his breath, felt that breath harsh and hot on her neck. He hooked his fingers in the band of black lace that held her panties on her hips and pulled them down. "Open," he muttered, pulling her legs wider, shoving his thigh higher between them. "Open for me."

She did. Oh, how she needed to turn, to hold him, kiss him, as she took him inside her. But he wasn't finished with doing things his way, no, his hand was all he gave her, his fingers—hard, clever, tormenting fingers. They teased for a few moments, playing lightly with her secrets, then slid inside.

She jerked. And moved involuntarily. Unaware, even, that she was moving with the thrusts of his hand, beyond caring about anything except what he was doing to her, giving to her. If it wasn't enough, it was still too much—sensations so rich and unsteady she could do nothing but cry out as she hit the sudden peak, convulsing around his moving fingers.

Slowly, slowly the world spun back into focus. Little tremors of unfinished pleasure still pulsed through her, and her chest heaved as she fought to take in enough air to clear her head.

His chest heaved, too. His breath was ragged, and his hands on her waist trembled. Though she'd wanted her pleasure to come with him inside her, she couldn't regret the wild ride he'd given her. Nor could she deny him one second's worth of whatever she could give him in return. She started to turn in his arms.

"No." His hands slid to her arms. Steadying her. Keeping her from moving. "Give me a minute. I'm not—stable—yet."

"Stability," she said, rubbing her head against his chest, "is all very well in its place. This isn't it."

"Cassie..." His breath shuddered through him. Then he shifted, removing his leg from between hers, and though he dropped his head to hers so that she felt his words against her hair as he spoke them, his hands held her a few inches away from his body. "Don't make this any harder on me than it already is."

What was he talking about? She shook her head, still dazed with the passion he'd called up in her, not sated in spite of the peak he'd hurled her into. Then he started to pull up the bodice of her gown.

Understanding struck like a fist. Gideon wasn't going to make love to her. Not fully. He'd changed his mind...again. She shoved his hand away.

Hastily she straightened her clothing, pulling up her panties, trying to get her shaky fingers to fasten the rhinestone clasp that held the dress up on her shoulder. The tears burning her eyes made her glad now that her back was to him. She didn't know how she was going to be able to stand looking at him— riding home in the car with him—oh, how could she live with him when he could switch himself on and off like that? When he could go from wanting her, needing her, to casually setting her aside like a jacket he'd tried on and then decided didn't suit, after all?

He moved away from the door. "Here," he said, reaching for the clasp her hands fumbled with. "Let me help you with that."

"Don't touch me."

"Hey." He put his hand under her chin and forced her head up. She glared at him. "If anyone has reason to cry right now, it's me."

He didn't look...casual. He looked strained and tight as hell. She bit her lip. "Why?" she whispered.

"I do know what birth control pills look like, Cassie, and I haven't seen any at the apartment. And I don't have any protection with me." Already the strain, like the blazing need she'd seen only too briefly, was leaving his face as he rebuilt his control. "I've no desire to risk disaster for a few moments of sex, however glorious."

Wounded, she stepped back. "Would it be such a disaster if I got pregnant?"

Gideon had finished reassembling himself. The cool, detached man she saw now little resembled the madman who'd dragged her in here. "Of course it would be," he said with chilly, devastating simplicity.

Ten

She was afraid she was pregnant.

Nine days late, Cassie told herself a week after the party, isn't really significant. Even though she'd always been as regular as the electric bill. She frowned at the large sheet of glass that she used as a palette. More cerulean blue, she thought, blending the gob on her palette knife into the shade of purple she was building. She wanted a dark, brooding sort of purple, but not too grayed down. Beneath the darkness should be plenty of life.

It's probably just stress. Everyone knew that stress could throw a woman's cycle off, and hadn't she experienced all sorts of stress lately? Somewhere she'd read that moving was among the top ten stress inducers. She couldn't remember where getting married fell in the ranking, but it was bound to be high. She'd certainly found marriage pretty stressful so far.

Afternoon light streamed in the undraped windows of the small bedroom she'd made her studio. Sunshine coated the tarp beneath her feet, the cluttered table beside her and Cassie's bare arms. Afternoon light, Cassie thought as she added the cerulean, was great for mixing colors, but lousy for setting the mood for the painting she planned. A thunderstorm would be about right, she thought, her hand resting unconsciously on her stomach. Especially one that belched hail and tornadoes.

She'd set aside her unfinished city scene. Another painting was building inside her, pushing at her too hard to ignore or postpone. A series of paintings, maybe. People, of course— Cassie usually painted people. But she was aiming for the archetypal this time rather than the ordinary. This painting would feature the face and hands of a young woman, her expression so calm it took on the aspect of a mask. But the woman's flowing robe, the way its screaming purple and dark-of-the-soul blues swirled around, weaving in and out of the near black background, would be Cassie's vision of Fear.

She loaded her brush with the purple she'd mixed, turned to the big canvas waiting on her easel and began.

Today she had no trouble losing herself in her work. So little trouble, in fact, that when she heard Gideon's voice behind her several hours later she jumped. "Oh," she said, turning, her hand resting on her chest where her heart still fluttered wildly. "You startled me."

Gideon stood in the doorway, looking crisply masculine in his dark suit and spotlessly white shirt. He'd already loosened the knot of his tie, and the sight of it half-undone sent a ripple of pleasure through her.

He glanced from her to the canvas she'd worked on all afternoon. A frown gathered above his dark eyes. "That's not like other paintings of yours I've seen."

"No, I..." Cassie made herself drop her hand and wished she could make her heartbeat behave. "I wanted to try something different." She glanced at the canvas, covered now in rough, swirling shades of darkness. The woman's face and hands were still unpainted and starkly white. What, she wondered, did Gideon see when he looked at it?

Too much, probably. "How late am I?" she asked brightly, dabbing her brush in the big coffee can that held her solvent, and standing so that her body blocked his view of her painting. "Will I still have time for a shower?" They were going out. Again. For the sixth night in a row. Every night since the party, in fact, they'd gone out on what could only be called dates—and every night they'd gone with another couple or in a crowd of people. Not alone.

"Oh, I think so. If you don't take too long opening this." He reached into the hallway behind him and held out a rumpled Neiman-Marcus bag.

Her breath caught. Another gift? He'd brought her a bouquet the day before yesterday. Not the kind that a man had his secretary order, either—a "bouquet" of three helium balloons tied to a handful of lollipop "flowers." And now— "Give it here," she demanded, happiness rising in her with the unstoppable effervescence of bubbles in soda pop.

"You'd better get some of the paint off first," he said, smiling as if, in spite of the streaks and smears of paint decorating her everywhere, he saw something splendid and rare when he looked at her.

Happily, hastily, she scooped solvent up in her palm, rubbed it over her hands and up her arm where a particularly bright streak of alizarin caught her attention, then wiped off with the cleanest rag she could find. "Stay right there," she instructed him, dashing to the hall bathroom to wash off the solvent. "I'll be right back."

Things had changed between them. Right after the party things had changed...for the better. She'd expected the opposite. Gideon had, after all, come very near to losing control in that bedroom when he'd claimed her with his touch. Before that night the threat of losing control had always made him retreat, shoving his feelings into deep-freeze. For some reason it was different this time.

For some reason Gideon was courting her. "Okay," she said, spinning away from the sink. "Give me my present."

He was right there in the bathroom doorway, holding out the wrinkled shopping bag. Just the sight of that bag made her heart swell, because it proved he'd picked out this gift, whatever it was, himself. If he had used the phone and a charge card, the present would have been professionally gift-wrapped, not stuck in a shopping bag.

With all the anticipation of a child on Christmas morning, she opened the sack. "Oh…" She lifted out her prize.

It was a spider. A fuzzy pink spider the size of a throw pillow and as soft as a lady's fur coat, with long, dangly legs and fat black eyelashes that drooped languorously over purple eyes. "Oh, she's gorgeous." Cassie hugged it to her. "I love her."

Gideon looked pleased and mildly embarrassed. "It reminded me of you."

"Did she?" Cassie turned her present to study the spider's come-hither expression. Her lips twitched. "Very sexy," she agreed.

"With miles of legs," he added.

Their eyes met. The spark that flew between them was easily identified, not so easily resisted. She knew, oh, now she knew, how much heat and purely physical pleasure he could bring her. And he knew—he must know—how easily he could cross the fragile boundary she'd set between them. How easily he could have what the sudden tightness in his face, the storm at the back of his eyes, told her he wanted.

But for six days and six nights—ever since the party—he hadn't touched her.

Maybe it was guilt. Maybe that's all that their dates and the gifts indicated—that Gideon felt guilty. For the hurt he'd already done her at the party. For the hurt he thought he would eventually give her. Cassie knew she wasn't any good at hiding her feelings. Maybe—probably—he knew more about what she felt for him than she wanted him to.

But…he might feel something other than guilt, something stronger, something, perhaps, as tough and tenuous as hope. Maybe Gideon *had* guessed that she was crazy in love with him…and wanted her to feel that way. Maybe he wanted gentle warmth as well as the dazzling heat, and craved the belonging that she longed to give him, and that's why he was offering her time spent together, little gifts that he'd picked out himself—pieces of himself, instead of the splendid flash fire of passion. She had, after all, told him she wanted them to know each other better before being intimate. He didn't know she'd changed her mind, that she'd planned to seduce him on the night he'd seduced her.

Maybe.

With so much, so very much, to hope for, how could she believe that being nine days late meant anything? He was looking at her again in the way that excited her—intent, absorbed, as if her face and her body held secrets he was determined to learn. "I'd better take my shower," she said, breathless.

His gaze slid over her body slowly, lighting little fires. "You do that," he said at last. And though he didn't say anything more, she knew she was running out of time. Gideon wouldn't keep his distance much longer, and when he did touch her again...

Soon, his eyes said. Soon.

He turned and walked away. She leaned against the lavatory, shaken, aching. Soon she would have to deal with the question she tried so hard not to think about. Because she couldn't go to his arms and his bed while keeping such a secret from him. Yet if she could just have a few more days, she told herself, she would probably be able to laugh at her worries. Nine days wasn't so long....

She turned on the shower, stripped and stepped beneath the water.

Gideon didn't want to give her a child, and of course he assumed there was no chance that it had already happened, so what would he think if...*no,* she told herself. No, she wasn't going to plan or panic or even think about it yet. Not yet, not when everything was going so well at last.

She applied her makeup with more haste than usual, went to her room and dressed. They were going with Ryan and his date to the club where Jaya sang, and that was all Cassie intended to think about. But on the way to the living area she paused by the door to her studio and looked at the big canvas with the dark, swirling colors.

It needed something more than the rather gothic colors she'd mixed so far. Fear had a shock of the unreal, something that would flash, hot and bright, through the somber colors, an unquiet shade that conveyed visually the feel of fingernails on a chalkboard. Maybe a lurid pink or a stomach-churning shade of chartreuse. A grab-you-by-the-throat color.

Her hand went to her own throat, where a tightness had lived ever since she realized her period was late. One time, she thought. They'd only made love once, on their wedding night, and though it was true they hadn't used protection, surely life couldn't be so capricious. Panic, she assured herself, never solved a thing. She had a few more days before she had to seriously consider the possibility that she had actually conceived that night in Las Vegas...the wedding night that Gideon didn't remember. The one she'd told him hadn't happened.

Determinedly she turned away from the big, waiting canvas. She didn't notice the way her left hand rested protectively over her flat stomach as she took a deep breath and walked down the short hall to her husband.

"I can wait a few more days," Cassie insisted stubbornly.

"No way." Jaya parked her aging, temperamental sports car next to the drugstore that was her goal. "Maybe I can't make you see the doctor, but you are taking one of those home tests if I have to lock you in the closet until your bladder gives you no choice."

Telling Jaya last night during her friend's break had been a mistake, Cassie conceded glumly as Jaya climbed out of the little two-seater. She should have known Jaya wouldn't stop at nagging, that she'd drag Cassie, kicking and screaming if necessary, into the harsh light of reality.

Reality, in this case, was Bidderman's Drugstore.

Cassie *had* known how Jaya would react, she admitted with a sigh as she, too, climbed out of the low-slung car. It didn't please her to realize she'd told her friend mainly so Jaya could bully her into doing what she should have done on her own. "Okay," she said to the skinny woman with the worried eyes waiting impatiently by the car. "I surrender. I'll go quietly."

"Listen, buying the test kit doesn't make you any more or any less pregnant." Jaya's words weren't sympathetic, but her eyes were. With one of her quick gestures, she grabbed Cassie's hands. "Maybe you'll find out you've been worrying for nothing."

"Maybe." Cassie glanced around. They'd come to an aging corner drugstore not far from Cassie's old apartment because she thought Bidderman's would be less intimidating than one of the cookie-cutter chain stores. The parking lot was nearly empty this early, although a blue sedan had pulled in a few minutes ago. Its driver still sat behind the wheel, hunting for something in the glove compartment. The old-fashioned store with its slower pace and touches of shabbiness made Cassie think of families.

Her hand touched her stomach once, lightly. "I think we can skip the part about locking me in the closet."

"Good." Jaya dropped her hands. "You know I'll be there for you, don't you? No matter what. And if you wind up having to give that man you married some news..." She frowned fiercely. "If he doesn't believe he's the daddy, I'll come over and shoot him, okay?"

Cassie's laugh may have been a little shaky, but the humor was real. So was the emotion that made her eyes fill. "Thanks." She squeezed Jaya's arm, then linked her own through it. "Come on. Let's get this over with."

Storms of weeping blue and violent purple raged around the woman with the pale, blank face. Cassie had chosen to leave the woman's complexion stark, her features strong but bleached of color, her eyes looking into a distance only she saw. Her hand—one of her hands—clutched at the robes that flew wildly in the tempest of dark colors.

But the color Cassie loaded her brush with wasn't a gothic

purple or brooding blue, nor was it the jarring shade she'd originally intended to highlight the figure with. The color on her brush, like the little licks of color she'd carefully painted in here and there, was green.

Spring green. The color of new life.

Cassie paused to smile at the woman on the canvas whose right hand clutched at the storm while her other hand rested firmly, protectively, over her womb.

Funny how wrong she could be. An hour ago she'd stood in the bathroom looking down at the little tester that spelled out her fate—a stick with two lines on it. One line, according to the instructions on the box, meant no. Two lines meant yes.

After one moment of blind panic while the shape of her world changed, Cassie had smiled.

A baby. She was going to have Gideon's baby.

How could that be a disaster? Gideon was wrong, she assured herself with a little nod, as she touched the edge of the woman's sleeve with the bright hope of spring. And she'd been wrong, too. She'd been so busy worrying about how Gideon would react to fatherhood that she'd ignored the fact that this pregnancy was happening to *her*. This would be her baby, not just his.

And she wanted it. Motherhood was new and frightening territory for her, but she did want this baby. She would just have to loan Gideon a little of her own joy until he understood their baby was a wonder, not a tragedy.

Not that she was fooling herself into thinking that everything was fine. Gideon was apt to be...difficult. Even after they got past those first few rocky moments when he absorbed the news, there was a chance he'd feel she'd tricked him. She had, after all, married him when he was drunk, lied to him about the consummation of their marriage, and now she was pregnant...a man less fair than Gideon, she conceded, might wonder if she'd gotten pregnant on purpose to trap him.

He might even wonder—just for a minute or two, she assured herself—if the child was his.

The doorbell rang.

Since she wasn't expecting anyone, she considered ignoring it. She didn't much want to stop painting. The doorbell chimed a second time. Reluctantly she cleaned her brush and set it aside. Whoever it was, they couldn't have gotten to the front door without being passed by the building's security, which meant the caller was one of the people on their list of approved visitors. She'd better go see who was here.

"Oh," she said in mild surprise as she swung the door wide. "Hello. Can I help you?"

A man who had probably once been handsome stood in front of her door, smiling at her with a strangely familiar face—strange, because she realized that, in spite of the odd sense of familiarity, she'd never seen him before. He wore a shabby gray overcoat and dusty loafers. His face was creased from years of hard living, and the dramatic white streaks in his black hair gave him a stagy look.

Maybe it was his eyes that gave her the creeps. The pupils were dark, the whites were vaguely yellowed and unhealthy, and they watched her, those eyes, far too intently. Her fingers tightened on the edge of the door.

"Hello, my dear," he said at last, smiling widely with his mouth. Only with his mouth. "Don't you have a hug for your father-in-law?"

Gideon knew who waited for him on the fifth floor. Building security had standing instructions regarding this one visitor— admit him, but notify Gideon as soon as possible. The emotions that sent Gideon racing up the stairs—emotions too close to explosion for the civilized confinement of the elevator— were as familiar as the deceit he'd lived with for twenty-two years.

Why in God's name hadn't he had the bastard removed from security's approved list? How could he have forgotten something so critical after he married Cassie? Sure, the old man hadn't showed up in a while—nearly four years now— but that was no excuse. Gideon knew from bitter experience that the old saying about how bad pennies keep turning up was simple truth. Now, because he'd allowed himself to forget, the one person Gideon truly hated was here. The old man must have seen the announcement in the paper and come here to his apartment. Where Cassie was.

Five flights of stairs weren't enough to make Gideon break into a sweat, yet when he reached the hall outside his apartment, he was sweating. He hadn't wanted Cassie to know. God, of all people, he hadn't wanted Cassie to know.

The moment the door swung open, he heard Cassie.

"Can I get you anything else?"

"No, no," said the voice he'd not heard in years. "Coffee is fine. And I don't mind waiting, not at all. It's been so long since..." A pause, punctuated with a sigh. "Now, don't be upset. I know Gideon tells people that I—well, that I'm not around anymore. You mustn't blame him." Sorrow touched the smooth baritone voice, a hint of wistfulness. "He has his reasons. I...wasn't always the best of fathers."

Gideon stepped inside, closing the door behind him. The noise was enough to alert the two people seated, one on each couch, in the living area. They both looked at him. Cassie was wearing baggy shorts, a huge, paint-daubed T-shirt and a tight little smile. The other person...

If only it weren't so much like looking in a mirror that mysteriously added thirty years, Gideon thought. Because the sight of the man was enough by itself to damage Gideon's control, and because he knew Timothy Wilde wouldn't be content with such small damage, Gideon was abrupt. "How much will it take this time?" he demanded.

The other man set down the coffee cup he held and stood. "Gideon." The dark, too-similar eyes in their network of wrinkles softened. "It's good to see you, son."

Gideon clamped down on the fury building inside. "Can't resist playing to an audience, can you?" Cassie's wide, worried eyes made it clear he had one. Gideon walked forward, stopping an arm's length from the man who had sired him. He should, he thought, have been able to smell the bastard from here—a stink like the slimy trail a slug leaves in its wake.

"If you ever," he said softly, "come around bothering my wife again when I'm not here, I'll see that you regret it for a long, long time."

Cassie jumped to her feet. "Gideon, he didn't—"

He sliced her a look that stopped her in mid-sentence. "Later." Then he said to his father, "Don't get greedy. You've sized her up and decided she's a soft touch, and you're right. That's why you'll stay away. Because if I learn that you tried bleeding her the way you've bled me for years, you'll lose more than the chance to extort money from me. I know how you operate, and I can learn more, old man, and I'll see you behind bars...again."

The old man's neck bowed slightly. "Whatever you say, Gideon."

A muscle jumped in Gideon's jaw. "Give it up, if you want to leave here with any of my money today. And that is what you came here for, isn't it?"

It was like seeing an actor wipe off the greasepaint. Timothy Wilde bent to retrieve the coffee cup he'd set down when his son walked in. When he straightened, his shoulders were firm, his head erect and his expression sharp. The dark eyes were now clear, so clear they no longer seemed to hold any feeling at all. He shrugged. "She wasn't really buying it, anyway. Oh, she was upset because she thought she should like me—such a pathetic old man. She felt sorry for me, but she couldn't relax." He frowned slightly. "Either I'm losing my touch, or you've married a clever woman."

Cassie had trouble believing her eyes. Or her ears. She hadn't felt comfortable with the seedy old man who'd shown up on her doorstep, but his transformation into this sardonic stranger shook her.

"I'm afraid I've shocked your wife." The voice was the same, but the tone was now lightly mocking. "My apologies, Cassandra. But you were so very ready to think the best of me that I couldn't resist. Women do enjoy feeling sorry for the men in their lives."

Gideon's voice sent a shiver down Cassie's spine. "But you're not in her life. You would do well to remember that."

Timothy Wilde took one long sip of his coffee, studying his son out of those eyes so eerily similar to Gideon's—and so completely different. "Thirty thousand," he said pleasantly, "for two years that you won't have to so much as hear my voice."

"You're incapable of keeping your word for two years."

The older man shrugged. "Twenty thousand, then, for one year."

Cassie desperately wanted to say something. But what? Maybe if she'd been prepared, she could have done something more than stand there, staring in appalled silence while Gideon negotiated the cost of his father's continued absence from his life.

To be prepared, of course, she would have had to know that Gideon's father was alive.

It didn't take long. They settled the fee for a year's disappearance at fifteen thousand. Timothy Wilde would pick it up at Gideon's office tomorrow—under another name. Cassie hugged her arms around her, cold all the way through, as she watched the man who was supposed to be dead walk out the door.

The door closed. Gideon turned to look at her. His expression told her little, but his body spoke of emotions brutally reined in. His jaw and his fists were clenched, his shoulders rigid.

"Talk to me," she said, holding her middle as if she could keep some traces of warmth from seeping away. "Tell me why you lied."

"Isn't it obvious?" His voice was low and savage. "I don't want that piece of garbage associated with me."

"But..." She swallowed. She'd known there was a great deal of himself Gideon kept walled away. She hadn't know how much. It hurt, learning he'd trusted her so little. "Does Ryan know about your father?"

He shot her a quick glance before stalking over to the bar.

"Afraid your brother has been lying to you, as well? Don't worry. I've kept the truth from Ryan, too." He grabbed a bottle from underneath the bar. "Care to join me? No? Well, you may as well realize that there's more than one similarity between me and the piece of slime who just left. We both lie, and occasionally I, too, need a drink." He slid a glass from the overhead rack and poured himself a shot of Scotch.

Cassie heard the savagery of pain, long held and never healed, in his voice. Unnoticed, her arms loosened around her middle as the need to go to him shivered through her. "I don't think you need a drink," she said as steadily as she could. "I think you need to prove that you can have a drink. Just one. And then stop."

For a second he froze. "But I don't always stop, do I? Or have you forgotten our wedding night the way I have? In that, too, I'm like him." Gideon toasted her with the glass, then downed the liquor in one swallow. "Even his drinking has never been predictable. But his sobriety today was no surprise. He knows better than to try and squeeze money out of me if he shows up drunk."

She should back off. She knew he wanted her to, and given the mood he was in, he would almost certainly hurt her if she pushed, lashing out the way any beast in pain might do. Cassie was no fool. She knew when to back off.

She started toward him. "You didn't answer my question."

"I didn't hear you ask one." He studied the empty glass he held as if he were considering refilling it.

She was crazy. That was the only explanation. "Why did you lie? Not just to me...to everyone. For years." Seeing him bitter and hating and hurting had made her crazy, and she couldn't help herself because all she could think about was helping him.

"I was ashamed." He slammed the glass down on the bar. "Is that what you wanted to hear?"

"No, because it isn't the truth." Shaky, she stopped in front of him. "Not all of it, anyway. You're the most honest person

I know, Gideon. You don't lie or cut corners or go back on your word.''

"Cassie." His face went tight, his eyes closing briefly as if he were in pain. When they opened again, the blaze she saw startled her. Amazed her. And woke her own heat, the beast that kept her awake at night, aching and alone as it prowled through her body with restless cravings. She sucked in her breath.

He seized her shoulders, staring down into her eyes. "For God's sake, woman, don't you have any sense of self-preservation? I'm no plaster saint. I'm rude and selfish and—''

"And strong and honest and—''

"Quit it. For God's sake, quit fooling yourself. You're going to get hurt, little girl, if you don't stop wandering around with stars in your eyes, working so damned hard at convincing yourself you're in love with me!"

Cassie flinched. Her heart pounded as if she'd just run, and lost, a race. Her palms were clammy, her mouth was dry, and it took a conscious effort to suck in a breath of air.

But her chin came up. Maybe her hands shook when she spoke, but her voice didn't. "Do you think I'm stupid enough to *talk* myself into loving you? That would be really bright of me, when all you want is to have sex with me for a year— though you'd prefer it just be for six months. Oh, and you're going to give me some money, too. Now that ought to make me wild for you." She tried to pull away from him, but his hands still gripped her shoulders as tightly as a miser holds on to gold.

"Cassie—''

"Shut *up*." She shoved at his stubborn, unmoving hands. "Sex and money, that's what you're offering—and then, in a year, we can get a nice, friendly divorce so my brother won't be upset. You think that's enough to make me *want* to fall in love with you? Well, even if I were stupid enough to think that a year's worth of lust was a good basis for falling in love, I know the difference between loving and wanting to be in

love, because that's how I lost my virginity, by wanting to be
in love with someone other than you, so I—''

He kissed her.

Not hard. Soft. That, as much as the shock of desire and
the pure pleasure of his mouth, silenced her brain along with
her mouth. He kissed her gently. Carefully. His lips moved on
hers as if he had all the time in the world for this kiss, and
nothing, absolutely nothing, that he wanted to do other than
lavish her mouth with attention, gently tickle her lips with his
tongue. As if he felt nothing more than the sweetest pleasure
himself, nothing stronger or darker, and had no needs of his
own, nothing except the craving to please her with his mouth.

If she hadn't felt the tension in the hands still clutching her
shoulders, she might have believed that lying kiss.

''Oh...'' she said, dizzy, when his head lifted slightly. His
mouth hovered, warm and wet and exciting, a few inches
above her own. How could he do this to her? How could he
make her fall even deeper in love with him when it should
have been her turn to make him fall in love with her? ''This
is not fair, Gideon.'' Her hands had slid under his suit coat
when she wasn't watching. They rested near his waist, and his
cotton shirt did nothing to keep his heat decently to himself.
Her needy hands clutched at him.

''I know,'' he said, and the terrible man stroked her cheek
then, his eyes and voice gentle while his hands trembled with
the ferocity of his restraint. ''I know it isn't fair, but I need
you, Cassie. I need you in my bed. Will you let me make love
to you?''

''Well,'' she said, trembling herself with wonder and greed,
''I guess that would be all right. If you'll let me make love
to you, too.''

A ghost of humor softened the wildness in his eyes.
''Deal,'' he said, and scooped her up off the floor into his
arms.

''Hey!'' It felt peculiar, being held high off the ground by
his strong arms, high against his chest, while he strode toward

his bedroom. Peculiar, but wonderful. She turned her head and licked his neck.

He made a strangled noise. "We're going to do this in a bed," he said, "so don't make me drop you. Quit that," he added when her mouth trailed up the taut cord in his neck.

"Okay." He tasted wonderful, musky and intoxicating. She traced the tip of her tongue back down his neck, but the layers of his suit, shirt, and tie frustrated her. "I can't wait to get some of these clothes off you." She thought about his chest—the muscles she'd seen on the morning after their wedding night, and the furry place right between his flat, dusky nipples—and squirmed. "Hurry."

He didn't drop her. Quite. At least, not until they reached the king-size bed, swathed in the early-evening shadows of his bedroom, and he went down with her when she fell. They locked together on the big bed, bodies tight and straining as they rolled, lips avidly seeking. She tugged on his tie, cursing it until she finally got the knot out and the first buttons on his shirt undone. He pulled on her shorts, popping the button off and jerking them down below her knees with one fierce sweep.

She kicked them off. His hand found the tiny triangle of lace covering her heat, and he groaned as he cupped her. "Cassie," he said, "tell me to go slow."

"Okay." Her mouth raced over his face and as much of his shoulder as she could reach, while her hasty fingers tried to get rid of his shirt and his suit coat at the same time. His hand kneaded her. She was dying. "Help me out here," she pleaded.

Between them, they managed to get his clothes off, destroying what remained of her reason in the process. Naked, large and implacably male, he seized her T-shirt and yanked it over her head, then pulled down her panties. Suddenly she was completely naked in the gathering darkness at the end of the day—naked before the storm about to take them both.

He turned away for the few seconds he needed to sheath himself in a condom. When he turned back and started to move on top of her, she trembled.

He froze. "Cassie." Carefully, as if she were a doe about to spook, he touched her face. His eyes were dark, liquid, luminous above her. "What is it? What's wrong?"

"Nothing." Yet she was shaking. She put both her hands on his chest, right where she'd imagined touching him. His chest hairs tickled her palms, his heat seeped into her, and she absorbed the frantic beat of his heart. How could she explain how overwhelming, how irrevocable, this was for her? She couldn't even think. Her own need pounded at her relentlessly. She raised her head and rubbed her cheek against the pelt on his chest, inhaling his scent. It helped. "I love you," she whispered.

He bent and gave her one of those deadly kisses again. The soft kind. A kiss that said he treasured her words, that maybe, just maybe, he needed to hear them as much as she needed to say them.

But their passion was too strong for the kiss to stay gentle. His tongue swept into her mouth, a delicious invader that sent her spiraling back into mindless pleasure. She moaned and lifted herself to him, but his body hovered inches too far away for her to get relief. He ran his hands over her body, stabbing his tongue into her mouth again and again, holding her still with those stroking hands as if he were determined to have her this way only.

The coil inside her wound tighter and tighter, until she was whimpering and gasping and fighting him for control of their lovemaking—until she thought she'd go over the edge from the sheer, tantalizing agony of his mouth on hers. Until at last he lowered his hands to her hips, lifted her, and, in one slick stroke, he thrust inside.

Inside her. Gideon was inside her, pounding himself into her, giving her his passion, his need, his body, his—

Cassie burst.

For a long, white-hot moment there was nothing—sensation so strong it blotted out everything. Then she was back inside herself, with little sizzles drizzling through her like electric confetti. Just as she remembered about breathing, Gideon found his own explosion. She heard her name on his lips as he followed her into oblivion.

His breath was loud in the quiet twilight of the room. So was hers. She lay on her back, smiling and smiling. He was heavy, but she didn't want him ever to move. Summoning all her concentration, she drifted her hand down his back, savoring the slickness of sweaty skin, the private, proprietary intimacy of touching her lover. "Hi, there," she murmured.

She felt his smile in the bunching of his cheek against her hair, though she couldn't see it. He shifted, slowly and not very much. Just enough so his elbows took some of his weight off her chest, and she had to admit that made breathing easier. "Hi, yourself," he said, his breath stirring her hair with each word. "You okay?"

She moved her head back and forth in tiny increments, just enough to qualify as a negative. "Nope. I don't think I survived."

"Pity." He moved again, apparently able to get more of his body parts functioning than she was. His neck held his head up enough for him to look down into her eyes, and his hand moved to cover her breast. "I hope you're wrong about that, since it would make what I've got in mind pretty kinky."

That surprised a laugh out of her. "Speaking of dead—or temporarily incapacitated—I don't think what you've got in mind is possible."

"Mmm," he said, and pressed his lower body against her while his thumb grazed her nipple, giving her another surprise, as fresh arousal rippled through her. She could see his face just clearly enough to know he was smiling. "But you made me too crazy, Cassie. I lost it. Instead of staying inside you a long time like I wanted to, moving inside you over and over, I went up in flames. So we have to try again, don't we?" He flicked her nipple with his thumb. "See if I can get it right."

"I guess," she said as she wrapped her arms around his neck, "I must have lived, after all. Maybe I ought to give you a chance to—'' Her breath sucked in when he pinched her nipple just hard enough to send a jagged bolt of heat from her breast to her groin. "To get it right.''

Eleven

Later, after Gideon had shown her just how right he could be, while they were still wrapped around each other, drained and wordlessly content, her stomach growled. He grinned, an expression that put her in mind of a wolf's cheerful menace, and sat up. "I'd better feed you. Got to keep your energy up. Stay where you are," he ordered, getting to his feet. "It's my turn to fix a meal for you."

"Mmm," she said, sprawled naked and happy in his bed. He flicked the light on as he left, giving her a great view of his bare backside, since he hadn't bothered to put a stitch of clothing on. She smiled. Maybe she should go help him? From what she could tell, Gideon had about the same degree of kitchen smarts as her mother. But that would rob him of the pleasure of giving, she decided. Even if all he came up with was some of that horrible sugary cereal in his pantry, it would be delicious. This was, she thought, the first time since their marriage that he'd wanted to do something for her that didn't involve money.

Well, not counting what he'd just done for her. To her. With her. She stretched, smugly savoring the aches in unaccustomed places.

He was gone fifteen minutes, too long for his menu plans to be as simple as pouring cereal and milk into bowls...and long enough for doubts to set in. Not doubts about what they'd given each other that evening, no, she couldn't regret a second of that. But she couldn't stop thinking. They'd made love twice. Both times she'd been out of her head for him and he'd been pretty far gone, too. Yet both times he'd retained enough presence of mind to use protection.

Gideon really didn't want to risk getting her pregnant.

Cold nibbled up her spine. She was going to have to tell him. Even now, especially now, when he'd truly begun to trust her, she couldn't leave a secret this huge between them.

He would feel trapped. Maybe tricked.

Then it will be up to me, she told herself stoutly, reaching down to pluck his shirt from the floor, to make him see things differently.

When he came back, magnificently naked, carrying a plate of sandwiches in one hand, wine and wineglasses in the other, she was primed to tell him. She really was. "My kind of man," she said when he set their meal on the bedside table. "Naked and bearing food." And speaking of food, which many primitive peoples associate with fertility...

"We'll explore your slave-and-master fantasies later," he said, and sat down beside her on the bed. His eyes silenced her before he spoke—dark, troubled eyes, a touch grim, more than a touch vulnerable. "Cassie. I owe you some explanations."

Apparently he'd had time to think, too. She laid her hand on his arm. "You owe me nothing."

He grimaced. "I owe you a damn sight more than explanations, but I don't know what to do about the rest. No," he said when she started to speak. "Let me get this said. You asked me why I lied about my father. I want to tell you."

"I think I've figured some of it out," she said gently.

"Your aunt started the story about his death, didn't she? Ryan told me years ago that your father died in an automobile accident and that he'd been drinking. Was there...did he go to jail, or something?"

"Or something," Gideon said grimly. "Prison."

She swallowed. "Yes, well, I imagine...Eleanor is rather ambitious, isn't she? And it must have been mortifying to have people know about her brother's failings."

"My aunt's life hasn't been easy. As a result, she's ambitious, yes—also obsessive about our family. She's become something of an amateur expert on genetics, especially theories about which traits are inherited, which aren't. You see, her father—my father's father—killed himself. Their grandfather's unpredictable rages resulted in two people crippled and his own commitment to a sanitarium. There are other stories. My family...isn't stable." His face tightened. "My father didn't just crash his car when he drove drunk that time, Cassie. He killed people."

Oh, dear God. Her fingers tightened on his arm.

Gideon stared straight ahead. "He ran another car off the road when he tried to pass. The driver was an old woman he thought was going too slow. She died at the hospital where my father was treated for a minor concussion." He paused, then went on very quietly. "My little brother Charlie was in the car with him. He was seven. He died without ever making it to the hospital."

Later, much later, Cassie lay alone in the quiet dark. Not physically alone. She was still in Gideon's bed, and he slept beside her, one arm draped across her hip.

She hadn't told him.

But how could she? When he'd had so much he needed to tell her?

He'd talked. For thirty or forty minutes he'd talked, and what he hadn't said in so many words she'd been able to piece together.

Gideon had been the one who took care of his brother. From

the time their mother died when Gideon was seven and Charlie
was two, Gideon had watched out for Charlie. It had been
Gideon who walked Charlie to school on the first day of kin-
dergarten. Their father might have bought Charlie his first two-
wheeler, but it was Charlie's big brother who had run along-
side the bike. When the little boy got sick, it was Gideon who
worried about getting the grape-flavored medicine because
Charlie wouldn't take the other stuff.

Timothy Wilde was a binge drinker. He would go for
weeks, sometimes months, without a problem, then he'd start
drinking and he wouldn't stop. One sunny day in October
twenty-two years ago, he'd quit the most recent of his jobs at
ten o'clock that morning and gone to a nearby bar. By the
time he decided to pick his youngest son up from school for
a trip to the movies, he'd been drunk.

Cassie didn't even try not to despise Gideon's father as she
lay in his bed. Her back was snuggled against Gideon's front,
the heat from his body wrapping her in a comfort that was
almost enough to soothe her into sleep. But she did make the
effort not to hate his aunt.

It wasn't just the lie. That had created all sorts of problems,
of course. Right after the accident, Eleanor Wilde had decided
it would be best if others thought that Gideon's father had
died in the crash. Gideon hadn't argued. At the time he had
wished it *was* his father who'd died instead of the brother he'd
adored.

Timothy Wilde had gone to prison for vehicular manslaugh-
ter. When he got out, he'd accepted the money his sister offered him to disappear. Later, the lie had become habitual for
Gideon, a matter of protecting his aunt from the distress her
brother caused her...and a way for Timothy Wilde to blackmail his son.

Yet the lie wasn't the worst of it. Eleanor Wilde had probably meant what she did for the best, Cassie told herself. And
Cassie could see how a woman with Eleanor's background
might decide she couldn't trust her emotions. It was still hard
to forgive Gideon's aunt for what she'd done to a twelve-year-

old boy who was crazy with rage and grief. Eleanor Wilde had offered her nephew a home, all right, and a degree of security Gideon had never known before. But her support had had strings attached.

From that day on, Gideon hadn't been allowed to have feelings. Emotions, wants, needs were the lures cast by madness in Eleanor Wilde's world and had to be suppressed, cast aside, ignored. To please her, Gideon had stopped talking about his brother, because he couldn't think of Charlie without emotions choking him. That suppression became habitual. By the time Gideon met Ryan, he honestly didn't know how to tell anyone that once he had had a brother.

Gideon's aunt had told the twelve-year-old boy she'd taken in that his only hope of avoiding the instability that ran in their family was to commit himself to unrelenting control. She had bent her efforts from that day on to see that he developed the necessary discipline.

But that wasn't all she'd done. Gideon didn't want to have children because he believed his blood was tainted.

Cassie lay awake in the dark for a long time, listening to the peaceful, even breathing of the man who had finally become her lover as well as her husband, and to her unquiet thoughts. Guilt was a vicious midnight companion, and one she was unused to entertaining.

She wanted to believe she'd kept her news to herself for Gideon's sake. But that wasn't true. Fear bound her tongue, not unselfish love.

How would Gideon deal with learning that the odds were good, very good, that he'd shortly have one more thing in common with the man he resembled and hated?

Fatherhood.

She threw up the next morning.

Gideon was so sweetly solicitous and so unsuspecting. Her guilt nearly killed her, but she let him persuade her to stay home from work. She was going to know beyond doubt, she'd decided, before she told him. She'd wait until a doctor confirmed the results of the home test.

Thirty minutes after Gideon left for work, Cassie hung up the phone, aggravated and panicky. Other people, she thought, have to wait weeks and weeks to get in to see a doctor. Not her. Not this time, at least. Her gynecologist had had a cancellation just before Cassie called, and her receptionist had been only too glad to offer Cassie the opening.

At eleven o'clock that morning.

When Eleanor Wilde hung up her phone at ten o'clock that morning, her hand was unsteady. Calm, she told herself. Be calm. Little by little, the dizzying influx of emotions brought on by the detective's news faded beneath the control she'd spent a lifetime perfecting.

Still, the depth of her fear was a datum to be noted and accounted for. And the fear was justified. After today, she would lose some or all of Gideon's affection. She knew better than most how little forgiveness was in him—she'd encouraged that trait, not wanting him to ever suffer his father's manipulations again. Now she must accept that he would, to a greater or lesser extent, turn against her. She couldn't let that stop her from doing what she had to do. For his sake.

Her hand was steady once more as she lifted the receiver and dialed Gideon's office. The detective's news offered her an unparalleled opportunity. And really, the chances were slim that the child Gideon's wife carried was his. Cassandra was trying to keep her pregnancy a secret, and secrecy equaled guilt, didn't it? Besides, the little tart wasn't even sleeping with her husband. Eleanor's detective had used the key to Gideon's apartment that she'd given him to determine that interesting fact.

The phone rang once at the other end. "Mrs. Pittinger," Eleanor Wilde said. "Put me through to my nephew, please."

Eleanor hadn't liked giving the detective that key, but it had turned out for the best. The man had checked the apartment more than once for anything incriminating, and he'd placed a listening device on the telephone. Then yesterday, after following Cassandra to another section of the city and a rundown drugstore, the detective had used the key to enter the apartment later and confirm what the druggist had reported—Cassandra's purchase of a home pregnancy test.

The bug on the phone had just provided additional confirmation.

"Gideon," Eleanor said as soon as she heard her nephew's voice, "allow me to be the first to congratulate you."

It was one of those rare, late-fall days when the sun puts on a spectacular farewell performance. Blue practically burst from the sky overhead. Down below, some trees dropped their leaves like strippers while others still clutched handfuls of orange, yellow and brown. The evergreens Cassie passed on her way home from the doctor's office were as darkly green as any ancient forest, and under the blessing of sun even the pale winter grass shone a glorious white gold.

Cassie drove carefully. She paused longer than usual at stop signs, feeling fragile and cautious and terrifyingly responsible. She watched the traffic, stayed within the speed limit, and signaled when she was supposed to. And when she parked her car and rode up in the elevator, she felt like laughing. Just laughing and laughing.

She was pregnant. Really, truly, beyond-a-doubt pregnant.

Her stomach was so flat. Cassie kept touching it, trying to detect a difference. It felt the same as ever, yet she was carrying a new life beneath her heart.

She would cook, she decided. She would fix Gideon a special meal, serve it to him with wine and candlelight, and she would tell him. And, she told herself fiercely as she put her key in the door, he would darn well get over his shock and his doubts quickly, and get happy. She'd see to it.

She was wrapped up in menus and a mental checklist of groceries, digging through her purse for her wallet to see how much cash she had, as she walked into the living area. She didn't see the two people who were already there, waiting on her.

"Cassie."

Gideon's voice startled her so badly she yelped. "Oh," she said, putting one hand to her chest, where her heart galloped. "You scared me to death. What are you doing home at this time of day? And Dr. Wilde," she said, belatedly noticing the woman who stood a few paces behind Gideon. She managed to smile, but really, this was a lousy time for Gideon's aunt to drop by. "I, uh, how nice to see you. Would you care for some tea? Or some lunch, maybe?" It was past lunchtime, and Cassie's stomach was mentioning the fact.

"Cassie," Gideon said again, and there was something frightening about his voice, something tight and dreadful. "My aunt came to me with...certain claims. I want you to tell me they aren't true."

Cassie felt the first crack of disaster opening beneath her feet. "What claims?" she said, and she wasn't hungry anymore. "What is it, Gideon?"

"I'll believe you," he said, and his eyes matched his voice—dark and intense. "If you tell me what she says isn't true, I'll believe you, Cassie."

Cassie looked mutely at Eleanor Wilde.

"I told Gideon about the child you're carrying," the woman said calmly. "The one you no doubt intend to pass off as his."

The world pitched violently, in one quick, sickening jerk.

"My aunt hired a detective," Gideon said in that terrible voice. "According to the detective, you were at the doctor's just now. He claims that he followed you there before calling my aunt. He claims that you knew about the pregnancy before today."

Panic was a cold beast. It wrapped chilly arms around Cassie's throat and chest and squeezed, breathing its poisonous vapors into her lungs. *This,* she understood with sudden clarity, *is all the chance I'm going to get.* If Gideon doesn't believe me now, accept what I tell him, trust me not to lie...

"Tell me the truth, Cassie," Gideon demanded.

What kind of marriage is possible without trust? "I did see a doctor today," Cassie said with desperate calm. "She confirmed that I am pregnant. And, Gideon—the child is yours. You know that. You *have* to know that."

The look in his eyes tore at her. She'd expected shock, anger—even, most painfully, doubt. She'd hadn't expected devastation. "One night?" he whispered. "You don't expect me to believe that, do you? How can you ask that of me, to believe that you would know you're pregnant after only one night?"

She felt a trembling start deep inside. "The one night that did it was our wedding night, not last night."

He said nothing. He didn't have to. His expression was so disbelieving she fell back a step. "Gideon—?"

"Come now, Cassandra," Eleanor said, as briskly as if she were speaking to a small child with a chocolate-smeared mouth who refused to admit stealing from the cookie jar. "You are only making matters harder on yourself and on Gideon by continuing this pretense. I can easily piece the story together. You are an adventuresome young woman. Perhaps you didn't plan to trick my nephew into marrying you when you first realized you were pregnant, but when he obligingly drank himself into a susceptible state, you didn't hesitate, did you?"

"No," Cassie said. "No, that's wrong, so wrong. Gideon, I know you don't believe what she's saying. You can't."

Gideon had no idea what he believed. Reality had started unraveling when his aunt had called. To *congratulate* him. Now, with Cassie confirming what his aunt had told him, reality lay in shreds around him. He grabbed at the tattered threads, trying to find some logical way to weave them back together, to make some sort of coherent whole of his world. "You can't know," he said slowly. "After making love one night, you couldn't know the next day that you conceived. Even a doctor can't tell that quickly." That was a fact. Wasn't it? He had to believe what the facts told him.

Cassie, his beautiful Cassie, was pregnant. The detective

said so, and she admitted it. She hadn't conceived last night, though.

Her child wasn't his.

"I did wonder if the father might be a married man," Eleanor said. "It would explain why he didn't claim you and the child. But that Armstrong fellow seems like a stronger possibility. He's trying to support himself with his art, so he has no money and probably little interest in having a family. And the two of you have been involved much longer than you've stayed interested in any of your other lovers, haven't you?"

Startlement flickered over Cassie's damnably ingenuous face. She laughed once, uncertainly. Damn her, she laughed. "Mo?" she said. "You can't be talking about me and Mo."

Armstrong had laughed, too, Gideon remembered. The man with the blond hair and the big nose had laughed while giving Cassie a ride on his shoulders on the day she moved into Gideon's apartment.

"My God," Gideon said slowly, soul-sick.

Tentatively she reached out, laying her hand on his arm. "I you're worried about your—your family history, just stop it Whatever your father is like, there's nothing wrong with you There won't be anything wrong with your baby. *You're no your father, Gideon.*"

He didn't speak. He couldn't. But he stepped back, so tha her hand fell away.

She flinched, but her chin came up. The hand he'd rejected spread over her belly in an age-old protective gesture. "Thi is your baby. You know that. You have to know that."

Gideon knew nothing. Even his pain was distant and be wildering. The facts kept swimming through his thoughts, slip pery as fish in water. He couldn't get his mind around the ide that his lovely mermaid had conceived another man's child— that she had planned to deceive Gideon into thinking that chil was his by marrying him, even taking him into her body. Pre tending passion for him, and more than passion.

Yet what else was he to think? "Does Ryan know?"

Cassie's voice, soft and terrible with tears, reached hir

dimly through the mists of unreality. "I haven't told anyone. Except Jaya. She…Gideon, you can't think I would lie to you about this."

Had their lovemaking last night been pretense? Another chunk of Gideon's world broke away, leaving him more alone in the void than he had ever been. Even at twelve, when he'd lost the one person who had mattered to him, he'd had his aunt to help him pull his world back into some sort of shape.

His aunt…who'd called to congratulate him today, even though she knew, due to her damned detective, that the baby couldn't be his.

"You have to tell me the truth," he said to his wife, forcing himself to see her pale face and the dull sheen of pain in her eyes. "The detective's report insinuated that you and this Armstrong were lovers, had been for years. It didn't matter, not really, not when it was in the past. But you have to tell me the truth now."

"Report?" Her voice was too high, like a guitar string stretched tight, ready to break. "Gideon—this detective wasn't your idea, was he? You didn't have me investigated—did you?"

He wasn't going to feel guilty, wasn't going to let her make him feel this crushing weight of blame. She was the one who owed him explanations—reasons, words, something to somehow make his world solid again.

Anger, even, would be a gift. He badly wanted to feel the anger he should be feeling. "No," he said, hardening his voice as he tried to harden his heart. "I didn't hire the detective. My aunt did. But his report listed your liaisons for the last few years, and Armstrong—"

"You read the report." Her voice had fallen, was utterly flat now. Empty, like her eyes suddenly were—chameleon's eyes with all the colors pressed out. "You read it, and you believed it. Just like now, you believe your aunt's poison and your own precious logic. Not me."

"If you tell me the truth now," Gideon said with irrational urgency, "I'll believe you." He wanted to, wanted desperately for her to convince him of something, anything, that he could hold on to.

She looked up at him out of those dreadful, colorless eyes. "I told you the truth. Didn't you hear me?"

She'd said it was his child. But it couldn't be.

Cassie shook her head, looking weary and...old. Terribly old. "Trusting me isn't very reasonable, is it? But I need you to trust me. I can't stay with you without that." She started to turn. Paused. "I'll be at Mo's place," she said softly. "I guess you've got the address, if you need to get in touch with me for anything. Your detective must have included it in his report." She turned and walked away.

The door closed behind her. He stared at that closed door, trying to think.

"Gideon," Eleanor said, "I know this hurts, but it's for the best."

Hurt? He felt nothing. Nothing at all.

Twelve

Seven hours after Cassie left him, Gideon sat alone on one of his leather couches. He hadn't bothered to turn any lamps on, and the bloody light from the setting sun tainted the whites and grays of his apartment and made the blacks seethe.

He wished like hell he was still numb the way he had been when the door had closed behind Cassie.

His album lay open on the couch beside him. A brown teddy bear with a plaid bow tie sat next to it. He'd looked through the album for the past two hours, reminding himself of what he wanted, what he needed, from life.

He had no idea why he'd brought the teddy bear out, too.

The raw pain that ate like acid at the lingering shreds of his earlier numbness bewildered Gideon. Why did he hurt this much? Why couldn't he think straight? He'd even driven by the old house where she used to live—the house where her lover lived now. The man she'd left him for. Like a teenager with a crush, he'd sat in his car outside on the street and looked at the lighted windows without once considering going

to the door and asking to see her. Even though that was what
he wanted above everything.

Yet how could he want that? Cassie had betrayed him,
hadn't she? Yet that wasn't what he *felt*. He felt, with irrational
conviction, that he was the one who had let her down in some
fundamental manner, not the other way around. Yet he
couldn't make the facts fit that certainty.

He thought he might be losing his mind.

"You're not your father, Gideon."

That's what Cassie had said, but what did she know about
it? He'd had to be so careful all his life. Careful with liquor.
Careful with the risks he took in business, limiting them to
only what he could rationally justify. Careful, certainly, with
his feelings...most of all, careful with women. With sex. He
didn't enter a woman unprotected. Ever. That might, he
thought, have been an admirable trait in another man, but in
his case it was purely selfish. The one risk he could never
justify was that of becoming a father.

"You're not your father, Gideon."

What the hell did she know? Gideon surged to his feet and
started to pace. His aunt knew him as well as anyone in this
world, and she certainly didn't trust him not to turn out like
his father. Oh, sometimes she told him she was pleased with
him. Once, when he graduated from college with honors, she'd
even used the word *proud*. That didn't stop her from watching
him as closely as a technician at a nuclear energy plant
watched his dials and gauges in the effort to avert disaster.

After Cassie had left, he'd told Aunt Eleanor to get out, too.

Eleanor had saved him from becoming a ward of the state
when he was twelve. She'd taught him how to fight his way
out of the misery of his childhood, taught him the value of
discipline and the necessity of having values. Yet at that moment he hadn't been able to stand looking at her. He wasn't
sure, now, if he ever wanted to see her again.

"You're not your father, Gideon."

Gideon's restless feet stopped by the big window. He stared
out. Night was falling outside in the blurry way it did in the

city, a creeping obscurity rather than true darkness. Few if any stars would break through both cloud cover and the competition offered by the city's millions of lights, and the clouds would reflect the city's lights back on it in a sullen, reddish haze.

The darkness in Gideon's apartment, though, grew more complete every moment. He wondered if Cassie was with Mo Armstrong right now. Talking with him. Cooking for him. Sleeping with him.

He didn't believe it.

"Hell." He put both hands on the window, fingers spread, leaning into the glass as if he could force reality into his mind by absorbing it through his body.

Cassie was pregnant. She said the baby was his, but it couldn't be. They'd only made love twice, both times the night before. Therefore, Cassie had lied and was continuing to lie to him.

He didn't believe it.

Gideon closed his eyes and rested his forehead against the cool glass. If the facts don't fit what you *know* to be true, that means you're losing your mind, doesn't it? Unless…unless you've made a mistake about your facts.

Vertigo struck so quickly Gideon staggered as he stepped back from the window. He shook his head. For a second he'd felt as if he were falling right through that glass. And maybe he had fallen through some sort of invisible barrier. The thoughts taking shape in his mind were glaringly obvious—yet he hadn't seen the obvious until this moment.

If he had made a mistake—if he was wrong about his facts—then Cassie was carrying his baby.

If he was wrong about the facts, then he'd practically forced her to leave him. If he was wrong…

If he was wrong, then he was going to be a father.

This time, when the monstrous fear swam up from the depths, he was too frozen by the chill of certainty to shove the beast back down without recognizing it. This time he saw the face of the monster. When it opened its jaws to swallow him, he smelled the rancid loathing of its breath.

The monster's name was Father, and its face was Gideon's own.

"You're not your father, Gideon."

If, Gideon thought, grappling in the darkness with his most deadly fear—if Cassie had told the truth about the baby, maybe she had told the truth about this, too. What if...what if fatherhood *didn't* turn him into his father?

What if he could have children? Would he fail them, too...as he'd failed Charlie?

Gideon turned, slowly. He stared across the darkened room, where he could faintly see the album against the paler darkness of the couch. There were no pictures of children in that album. Weddings, but no children. Pictures of houses, but no families.

No love.

Next to the album sat the darker blob that was the bear, the silly, childish teddy bear Cassie had given him that day at the carnival. He stared at the bear and the album, and he knew.

He *knew*. With his heart and his mind, with his intellect and his soul, he knew the only answer that really mattered.

Cassie sat out on the wooden steps leading to Mo's apartment. She'd been sipping orange juice in a wineglass and arguing for hours, watching while the shadows under the trees grew and merged with twilight. At first she'd argued with Mo, but she'd continued just fine on her own when he left to make a run to the store for groceries.

By the time the darkness was complete, though, she'd pretty much lost the argument. She just wasn't ready to admit it.

"I'm not testing him," she muttered at her wine. "I came to Mo because Mo is my friend, not because I wanted Gideon to prove anything."

Yeah, right. And that's why you never bothered to explain Mo's sexual preferences to your husband—because you weren't testing him.

Cassie sat in a dim puddle of light that leaked out from

around the blinds in Mo's apartment and scowled at her nearly empty wineglass. The voice in her head was a lot more sarcastic than Mo had been. He'd gently pointed out that testing your partner was a form of game playing, and it seldom worked. People don't react well when you try to make them prove themselves.

"But Gideon should have trusted me," Cassie whispered. "He should have known I would never do what he thinks I've done." Her eyes fogged with tears for the hundredth time since she'd banged on Mo's door that afternoon. Angrily she wiped the dampness away. "The stupid man wants me to prove myself to him, doesn't he?"

She knew she sounded angry at him. Was she testing Gideon—or punishing him?

If she'd intended to do either one, Cassie thought glumly, she'd sure fallen flat on her face. He hadn't come. She'd told Mo she was sitting outside because the weather was so pretty, not because she was waiting for Gideon to show up and prove that he cared and was sorry for doubting her. She'd told herself that, too. She believed it about as much as Mo had.

The sad cry of a mourning dove drifted down from the unseen branches of the biggest elm. Cassie sighed heavily and admitted the truth. She had decided to come to Mo instead of Jaya or her brother because, all stuffed with hurt and anger the way she'd been, she'd thought that Gideon didn't deserve to have her back unless he trusted her even when appearances counted against her.

Appearances like leaving him to stay with another man. Or being pregnant when she'd insisted that he never made love to her on their wedding night.

The anger was pretty much gone now, leaving just the hurt. She had a feeling that might be with her for a long, long time. He hadn't come. Oh, she tried telling herself that he might come in another day or week, but in Cassie's experience, time wasn't likely to help him change his mind. The passage of time just made a person more used to thinking whatever they'd been thinking and less interested in backing down.

The hurt was like a wailing inside her, a sharp slice of sound trapped inside.

"I'll do just fine," Cassie said, and nodded firmly at her glass. She'd done fine without Gideon before. She'd do even better now, because she'd have a baby—his baby—to love. She...

Was crying. Again. Dammit.

She squeezed her eyes very tightly closed for a moment so they would stop leaking. When she opened them, he was there. Gideon. In front of her. Halfway up the steps, but not moving. He stood there as frozen as a dream, staring up at her, his expression unreadable in the darkness.

She blinked. He was still there.

"Cassie," he said, then stopped. "Cassie," he said again, but her name told her no more this time than it had the first— told her nothing of his feelings, gave her no clue as to why he was here. But he was *here.*

He came up another few steps until his head was level with hers, and she saw his face. He scowled fiercely when he said, "You've been crying."

She stood up so she could look down at him. "No, I haven't."

"Yes, you have." In two strides he was level with her. Crowding her. "Dammit," he said, taking her shoulders, "don't you ever cry over me. I'm not—oh, God, Cassie." Abruptly his grip shifted and he pulled her closer, so close she had to tip her head back to see his face. "I'm not worth one of your tears, not one."

Shaky with doubt and hope, she frowned as ferociously as he did. "You are worth far more than a few tears. You are a stupid, stubborn, impossible man who is worth anything I could give, because you are also honorable, honest, dependable, strong—and you've got a ridiculously sexy body, and I—"

He wrapped both arms around her and squeezed her hard enough to make her squeak.

"Sorry," he muttered. "Oh, God, I am so sorry, Cassie.

For everything. For doubting you. For reading the detective's report. For letting you think for even a moment that I could let you go.''

"Does that mean you can't?'' she asked, her voice muffled by his shirt.

"Damn right,'' he said. "I didn't know, Cassie. I didn't understand what I felt around you, and I didn't trust it. All these years...I had to get roaring drunk before I could admit to wanting you in a way I've never wanted another woman. A permanent way. I had to get so drunk that I'd forget feeling that way, because I couldn't handle it.''

"Oh, well then...'' She had to pause to summon up courage, because everything he said was so wonderful she didn't want to question it, or him. But she had to. "Does that mean you believe me now? That you know whose child I'm carrying? Because this baby deserves a real father, Gideon.''

He released her from his bear hug and lifted his two big hands to cradle her face. He tipped it up to him and spoke softly, seriously. "It means that I love you, Cassie. I love you so much it wouldn't matter if you did carry another man's child. I'd still want it, and you. But yes, I believe you. That's what I couldn't stand, you see. I believed you all along, and it made me crazy because it seemed so crazy to believe what I *felt* instead of what I thought were the facts.''

He brushed his lips across hers again, sending tingles of hope up her spine and down her fingers. "You're having a baby,'' he said, his expression achingly tender. "My baby.''

Her heart stuttered madly. "Gideon.'' In the darkness of the night, sunlight was somehow leaking in under her skin. She shook her head, dizzy with wonder. "And you're okay about it? About being a father?''

"You explained things to me, but it took me a while to catch on.'' He smiled. "I'm not my father. I'm not going to turn into him by becoming a father myself. I don't know that I'll be any good at it, but...Cassie, I want this baby. I want it more than I've ever wanted anything. Except you.''

Such wisdom and courage ought to be rewarded. Cassie

gave herself that job and performed it with enough enthusiasm that she could barely stand a few moments later when he lifted his head. "Maybe," she said breathlessly, "we should finish this discussion at home."

"Home..." There was an odd, arrested note in his voice when he repeated the word, followed by what she could only call smugness. "Yeah. Home sounds good. Let's go home, Cassie."

"I should leave a note for Mo."

"You don't have to."

She frowned. "He'd worry, Gideon. He's at the store, but he'll be back at anytime, and—"

"No, he won't. Not until he sees us leaving." Gideon grinned. "I met him as I was pulling up in the driveway. It took a little doing, but I convinced him to wait to make an appearance until I'd had a chance to talk to you." He rubbed his cheek on the top of her head. "He's waiting at the end of the driveway, ready to come up and bash me a few times if I do anything wrong—or to wave us on our way."

Cassie loved it when he rubbed his cheek against her like a big cat. It did occur to her, though, that she had a confession to make. "About our wedding night," she began, and winced at the guilt she heard in her voice.

She felt the rumble of his chuckle as much as she heard it. "Lied, didn't you?"

She lifted her head to stare at him.

"It's the only logical conclusion," he said, stroking her hair. "Once I came to my senses and eliminated the impossible—that you would lie to me about whether the baby was mine—what remained was entirely possible. Probable, even, considering how angry you were that morning."

She frowned, not sure she liked the twist his stupid logic had taken. "Oh, so you think it's *probable* that I'd lie to you."

"I think," he said, pressing a kiss at the corner of her eye, "that you are a maddening, stubborn, impulsive, hot-tempered woman—" he caught her hand before she could punch him in the chest "—with an incredibly honest, generous heart, and the most loyalty, love and sheer, blinding courage of anyone I've ever known, and I will never let you go.''

"Well," she said, the sunlight inside her burning so brightly she thought he must be able to see it, "there's one other thing you should know."

"What's that?"

"I love you," she told him happily.

"Yes," he said, his voice soft with certainty. "I know."

Epilogue

Cassie woke slowly. Slowly but not reluctantly. Hardly that. She shivered as thick, masculine fingers left one breast to tease the other. Beyond the muscular shoulders that partially blocked her view she saw the pale, gilded colors of the luxury suite, looking dusky in the early morning light. "Cinderella's coach," she murmured.

"Hmm?" Gideon didn't seem interested in conversation. He appeared to favor continuing the activities of their wedding night.

Their *second* wedding night, almost six months after the first one.

"Our suite," she said, reaching up to drape her arms languidly around his neck. "It reminds me of Cinderella's coach, all cream and gold." Like the pirate's chest that sat at the foot of the bed and her bouquet—the same bouquet he'd given her the first time, dried now and fragile—that rested there.

He paused, his dark eyes intent on her face. "Is that good? You said you wanted the same suite."

"Oh, very good," she assured him, and they smiled at each other, aware of nothing except this moment when they held each other, warm and naked and in love. "So," she said, one hand sliding down to enjoy the hairy place on his chest, "how's your memory this morning? Do you recall anything about what we did last night?"

"I'm kind of fuzzy." He nibbled along the column of her throat, sending little shivers over her. "Maybe you could prompt me."

"Well," she said with a sigh as her hand went lower still, "if I must. At one point I did this."

He growled.

"Remember?" she asked sweetly.

"Let's see," he said, and tossed the covers off both of them. "Was that right before or right after I did this?" And he lowered his head to her breasts.

His lips were gentle on her sensitive nipples, but his tongue was wicked. It grew more wicked yet as he made his way over the mound of her stomach, where her "innie" belly button was turning into an "outie" as her pregnancy progressed.

"Ohh…" she said, clutching at his hair. "Are you sure you did that? To a pregnant lady? Now my memory's getting…oh, my…kind of fuzzy."

"Well," he said, moving between her legs, "maybe not. Maybe I did this, instead." And he hooked his hands under her knees, bending them and opening her wide, and he kissed her. Right *there*.

Cassie forgot about everything, absolutely everything, but the blinding glory of what his mouth did to her. Quickly, easily, he drove her up to the peak—and then made her tarry there for several frantic moments before sending her over. While she was still quivering, he put himself inside her and began to move.

Her second peak was gentler than the first but just as sweet, since this time she could watch him topple off the edge of reality, too.

He rolled to his side immediately afterward and held her

close. The drapes were open, letting them watch together in silent contentment as the morning gathered light and spread it over the golds and creams in the hotel suite.

After a few moments Cassie, unable to be still for long, rolled over to face him. He smiled, took her hand and brought it to his mouth. "My wife," he said softly, and kissed the shiny gold band he'd put there five months, three weeks and two days ago.

Her heart gave a happy jump. Gideon had used the same gesture last night, when they'd renewed their vows at one of the resort's wedding chapels. "With this ring I thee did wed," he'd said, and kissed the band he hadn't wanted her to remove, even for the ceremony. Then he'd continued, "With this ring I renew my promise to love, honor, cherish and trust you for all the days of our lives."

"It was a beautiful wedding," she whispered now.

Gideon had been determined to have a second wedding and wedding night, but he hadn't wanted it to replace their first wedding. No, perfectionist that he was, he'd just wanted to do it again and get it right. This time they'd had dozens of candles and a chapel instead of neon and a converted RV.

Because Cassie thought he should have a wedding *he* remembered, too, she hadn't argued. So this time he'd given her candlelight and promises, because now Gideon knew that not all promises about love were lies.

Her brother had been present again, but, unlike before, he hadn't been the only witness. Jaya and Mo had attended as the bride's guests. Mrs. Pittinger and Eleanor had sat on the groom's side.

Eleanor was now resigned to her nephew's marriage, if not happy about it. She was also quite desperate to retain some contact, some kind of relationship, with Gideon. Cassie could see that, even if Gideon couldn't, and, being who she was, Cassie had already forgiven Eleanor. Gideon was still struggling with forgiveness, but he was making progress.

Cassie intended to see that he kept right on with that progress.

He's learning, Cassie thought, playing with her husband's ear and breathing in the luscious warmth of his scent. However badly Eleanor had behaved, however poor a job she'd done of stepping in when Gideon was a boy, Cassie knew Eleanor did love her nephew, and Gideon needed to know it, too. To *feel* it, deep inside.

"Are you happy, Mrs. Wilde?" Gideon asked, his hand wandering once more to her breast.

"I'll do," she assured him.

His brows drew together. "I didn't get too rough, did I? The doctor did say it was okay to make love."

Cassie had not been surprised to learn that Gideon was hideously overprotective. "I'm fine," she said, and moved his hand to the mound of her stomach, where a tiny foot suddenly kicked. She smiled. "Archie and I are both fine."

"Lucy," he corrected her, smiling. Due to the baby's position during the sonogram, its sex remained a matter of hot debate. The doctor insisted it was a boy. Her nurse claimed it was definitely a girl. Cassie and Gideon had made a game of guessing. If one of them said Sally, the other automatically said Peter or Joshua.

Gideon cupped her belly with firm, warm fingers. "Cassie…"

She laid her hand over his and waited for him to continue.

"Tell me again," he said, "that you think I'll be okay at this fatherhood stuff."

"You'll be wonderful," she said softly. Gideon still couldn't bring himself to say he was afraid, but she knew he was. Once he'd faced his biggest fear—that of turning into his father—much of the bitterness and hatred he'd felt for the man had drained away, freeing him. But other fears lingered. "You took good care of Charlie, Gideon," she told him, repeating an assurance he needed to hear every so often. "What happened to him wasn't your fault in any way. You'll take good care of our child, too."

He was silent, his big body still and tense. Then, slowly, he relaxed. "Yes," he said, his voice husky. "Yes, I did take

care of him. At least I tried." His fingers slid up to her waist
in a slow caress. "Something occurred to me. About Charlie."

His hand started back down, which was dreadfully unfair if
he wanted her to pay attention to what he was saying.
"Hmm?"

"Charlie was a sunny child, bright and happy in spite of
being my father's son. So my aunt was wrong about what is,
and isn't, possible for the Wilde men."

"She certainly was." Just then Gideon's fingers reached the
tangle of fiery curls at the top of her thighs. And stopped. She
sucked in a breath. "Gideon?"

His palm rested warmly on the lower part of her stomach
while the tips of his fingers toyed with those curls. "I'm going
to want more than one child," he announced. "Which is just
as well, since you seem to get pregnant awfully easily. How
many children do you want me to give you, Cassie?"

"Lots," she said indistinctly as his fingers slid farther
down. "Though maybe we should practice awhile... Gideon?
You can't be ready yet."

"Mmm," he said, his mouth pressed to her neck as he lav-
ished attention on her with his fingers in the most delightful
way.

"Are you—oh, yes. Like that." She gathered her fading
resources of concentration and managed to say, "I did sort of
take advantage of you the first time we came here."

"Thank God," he said. "If you hadn't, I might have ended
up with the wrong wife."

"You weren't very bright about that sort of thing," she
agreed breathlessly. "You kept picking blondes."

"I've come to my senses. I like redheads much better
now," he assured her, and did his best to prove the truth of
his words.

*   *   *   *   *

In April 1997
Bestselling Author

DALLAS SCHULZE

takes her Family Circle series to new heights with

TESSA'S CHILD

In April 1997 Dallas Schulze brings readers a
brand-new, longer, out-of-series title featuring the
characters from her popular Family Circle miniseries.

When rancher Keefe Walker found Tessa Wyndham he
knew that she needed a man's protection—she was
pregnant, alone and on the run from a heartless past.
Keefe was also hiding from a dark past...but in one
overwhelming moment he and Tessa forged a family
bond that could never be broken.

Available in April wherever books are sold.

SILHOUETTE... Where Passion Lives

Order these Silhouette favorites today!
Now you can receive a discount by ordering two or more titles!

SD#05988	HUSBAND: OPTIONAL by Marie Ferrarella	$3.50 U.S. ☐	/$3.99 CAN. ☐
SD#76028	MIDNIGHT BRIDE by Barbara McCauley	$3.50 U.S. ☐	/$3.99 CAN. ☐
IM#07705	A COWBOY'S HEART by Doreen Roberts	$3.99 U.S. ☐	/$4.50 CAN. ☐
IM#07613	A QUESTION OF JUSTICE by Rachel Lee	$3.50 U.S. ☐	/$3.99 CAN. ☐
SSE#24018	FOR LOVE OF HER CHILD by Tracy Sinclair	$3.99 U.S. ☐	/$4.50CAN. ☐
SSE#24052	DADDY OF THE HOUSE by Diana Whitney	$3.99 U.S. ☐	/$4.50CAN. ☐
SR#19133	MAIL ORDER WIFE by Phyllis Halldorson	$3.25 U.S. ☐	/$3.75 CAN. ☐
SR#19158	DADDY ON THE RUN by Carla Cassidy	$3.25 U.S. ☐	/$3.75 CAN. ☐
YT#52014	HOW MUCH IS THAT COUPLE IN THE WINDOW? by Lori Herter	$3.50 U.S. ☐	/$3.99 CAN. ☐
YT#52015	IT HAPPENED ONE WEEK by JoAnn Ross	$3.50 U.S. ☐	/$3.99 CAN. ☐

(Limited quantities available on certain titles.)

TOTAL AMOUNT	$_____
DEDUCT: 10% DISCOUNT FOR 2+ BOOKS	$_____
POSTAGE & HANDLING	$_____
($1.00 for one book, 50¢ for each additional)	
APPLICABLE TAXES*	$_____
TOTAL PAYABLE	$_____
(check or money order—please do not send cash)	

To order, complete this form and send it, along with a check or money order for the total above, payable to Silhouette Books, to: **In the U.S.**: 3010 Walden Avenue, P.O. Box 9077, Buffalo, NY 14269-9077; **In Canada**: P.O. Box 636, Fort Erie, Ontario, L2A 5X3.

Name:_____

Address:_____ City:_____

State/Prov.:_____ Zip/Postal Code:_____

*New York residents remit applicable sales taxes.
Canadian residents remit applicable GST and provincial taxes.

SBACK-SN4

Silhouette ®

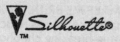

National Bestselling Author

MARY LYNN BAXTER

"Ms. Baxter's writing...strikes every chord within the
female spirit."
—Sandra Brown

LONE STAR
Heat

SHE is Juliana Reed, a prominent broadcast journalist whose
television show is about to be syndicated. Until the murder...

HE is Gates O'Brien, a high-ranking member of the
Texas Rangers, determined to forget about his ex-wife. He's
onto something bad....

Juliana and Gates are ex-spouses, unwillingly involved in an
explosive circle of political corruption, blackmail and murder.

In order to survive, they must overcome the pain of the past...and
the very demons that drove them apart.

Available in September 1997 at your favorite retail outlet.

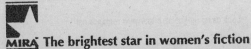